//TURBO_

///TRAILBLAZER

////////////

//TURBO RACERS//
TRAIL
BLAZER
BY AUSTIN_ASLAN

TURBO Racers: Trailblazer

 For information address HarperCollins Children's Books, a division of HarperCollins Publishers, 195 Broadway, New York, NY 10007.

www.harpercollinschildrens.com

Library of Congress Control Number: 2018954192

ISBN 978-0-06-274105-9

Typography by Joe Merkel

19 20 21 22 23 PC/BRR 10 9 8 7 6 5 4 3 2 1

❖

First paperback edition,2020

To my trailblazing son, Everest, ////////////////////
whose boundless enthusiasm,
natural wit, and utter self-confidence
have brought Mace Blazer to life.
By land, by air, and by sea,
may you soar always beyond your horizons,
and may you savor every adventure
you forge along the way.

CHAPTER ONE /////

Mace was tense in his seat, his palms sweaty. The checkered flag was on the horizon, growing large. Larger. He stole a glance to either side. No one near him. Just the gray blur of grandstands and stadium walls. But there was no time to lose. His foot fused to the gas pedal. The steering wheel rattled. Mace tightened his grip. The flag filled the windshield . . . then it was gone. *Yes! Nailed it!* Another first-place finish. No surprise there. But . . . his *time*? How fast? Had he beaten his previous record? Had he beaten it by enough?

The video screen cut to black. Mace held his breath as

the scores loaded. His foot hurt. He gave his leg a shake, feeling blood flow back into his clenched muscles.

It had been a flawless run, for sure. A virtual reenactment of the 2002 Nova Scotia Gauntlet Prix Qualifier. Mace had effortlessly transformed his vehicle into a roadster, an aircraft, and a torpedo-fast submarine. Unrelenting high speeds over ice, under sea. From the lineup he'd picked *Triassic,* an antique craft once piloted by famed TURBOnaut Rex Danger. Mace liked the older models. They felt less fragile. More stable. Less . . . *whiny.*

But his *time*? Had he pulled it off? If he'd shaved two seconds from his previous best score, he would retake the number-one slot on the global leaderboard.

That's right: *global.* As in: the world's best TURBOnaut.

Virtually speaking, at least.

The simulator's dashboard flashed. The hatch hissed. Fluorescent lighting from the arcade flooded the cockpit, and the sounds of other video games chimed in his ears. Somewhere beyond the clacking of a frantic air-hockey match, Pac-Man was dying. Dig Dug was digging. Q*bert was cursing. A wooden Skee-Ball ricocheted into a hole, and reward tickets belched from a printer.

A stab of joy took hold of Mace's chest. He loved the chaotic noises of the arcade.

The TURBO simulator finished opening. Its screens filled with names and numbers.

"Yes!"

MBlaze07 appeared at the very top of the list, right above a dude named Caballero.

"Take that, cowboy! And everyone else . . . In. The. World!"

As a prize, his stomach growled. He'd missed lunch entirely, but it had been worth it. The TURBO simulator was more than a game. The arcade was more than a hangout. He loved the crowds, the lights, but more than anything, he knew, he craved the lack of silence. He'd run out of allowance last week and had stayed away from the arcade. A rotten situation. He'd lost his first-place slot because of it.

But one good showing would put him back on top.

And he'd done it.

MBLAZE07.....................................#1

His time was lightning fast. It was almost unfair. Poor rest of the world. *Just look at that time . . .* Mace glanced at his watch. *Holy cow! Look at the time!*

Sixth period would start in eight minutes, and school

was at least fifteen minutes away from the mall.

Mace jumped up, banging his head on the underside of the simulator's plastic canopy. "Ow!" He tumbled from the cockpit to the arcade's linoleum floor, snatched up his backpack, and sprinted for the exit.

"Hey, Mace. Where've you been?"

Someone stepped in front of him before he could escape. One of the arcade employees. The guy was always tinkering with the TURBO simulator. The thing had about a million moving parts and was always in need of repair.

Mace dodged the guy. "I've got to get to class!"

"Hold on. Take this!" The man laughed, holding out a booklet. "There's a classic, first-gen TURBO racer in town. Today's the last day to see it at the museum. You should go check it out." The man's gaze was insistent, his eyebrows thick and black. "Seriously. Don't miss it."

"Thanks," Mace said, snatching up the pamphlet and tearing through the mall.

Cool, he thought as he ran. But if Mace didn't hightail it back to class, the only thing he'd be missing this afternoon would be his freedom. As in: detention.

School was uphill from the mall. Mace knew he didn't have a prayer.

He huffed and puffed his way up the mountain, through the tall pines. So much for being the fastest kid alive.

Five minutes too late, Mace barreled into sixth-period English class and skidded to a stop right at his seat.

Mrs. Arbuckle, writing on the whiteboard, never turned around. "Mace Blazer, that's your fifth lunch tardy this month. There's a detention referral waiting for you on the edge of my desk."

"Oh, but I'm not late," Mace said, catching his breath. "I was at the front desk. They were trying to get a hold of my mom. And, well, you know how that can be tricky sometimes."

Mace bit his lip. This was a new low for him. But detention was not an option.

"Ah." Mrs. Arbuckle turned, lowering her gaze as if she was trying to scan him for the truth. "Understandable, but bring an excuse slip with you next time that happens."

"Yes, ma'am," Mace said, his heart pounding in his chest. That was a risky move, but he'd come out ahead. All in a day's work.

"Yes, ma'am," parroted the boy behind Mace. "What a gentleman!" Carson Gerber. "Been down at the arcade again?"

The Gerb's anger had been simmering since third-period Spanish. He and Mace had been paired as partners, but Carson had stumbled over reading his script. *"¿Donde está el banjo?"*

"Uh, there's no *j*. I think you mean *baño*," Mace had offered. "But if it's so urgent, you could use a tuba in the music room."

"Gross!" a girl in the front row had protested.

Carson had turned lava red and promised to pound that extra *j* out of Mace.

Now, Carson whispered, "Well, I hope you enjoyed your *play*time. You know, my dad's a real 'naut. While your eyes bleed at the mall all summer, we'll be racing for reals—all over the globe."

Mace sighed. "Dude. Your dad's not a real TURBOnaut. He's hobby league."

"Are you making fun of your mom's boss now?"

Carson's dad owned the business where Mace's mom worked. She packaged and shipped the outdoor clothing his company sold online. Unlike Carson, Mr. Gerber was a nice guy—at least as far as Mace knew. "No, I'm making fun of you, Gerbs!"

"That's it, Blazer. You're toast!"

"Boys," Mrs. Arbuckle warned.

While his English teacher analyzed the results of the class *Black Stallion* test, Mace focused on a very different kind of racehorse. His eyes flew over the brochure from the arcade. The TURBO racer on the cover was pure black, shaped vaguely like a cross between a Frisbee and a football. The announcement made his heart rattle.

THE
EVENT HORIZON

FULLY RESTORED! • ON DISPLAY NOW!

An exhibition at the Colorado Museum of Aeronautics and Aerospace Engineering.

See the first-generation trimorpher.
One of the first vehicles of its kind, tackling land, air, and sea all in the same race—the **Event Horizon** *was destined for greatness, but crashed and burned ahead of its time.*

The legendary TURBO craft was in Boulder. Today was the exhibit's last day.

Mace had to see a real TURBO vehicle up close. No way he'd be able to focus on anything else until he did.

"What do you think, Mace?"

"Huh?" His neck snapped up. Mrs. Arbuckle was staring at him from the front of the classroom, her expression impatient. "You don't have one selected, do you? I can pick a topic for you."

Mace cleared his throat, gave his teacher a charming smile. "Um, what were you saying?"

"What're you reading there?"

"Oh, it's nothing," he tried.

But this wasn't nothing, he thought. The *Event Horizon*! In Boulder! An old classic, for sure. Much older than *Triassic*. A dream ride, no doubt.

"Hand it over, Mace." Mrs. Arbuckle's tone soured.

"Yes, ma'am." Mace lifted the brochure.

"What I'm interested in"—Mrs. Arbuckle held out her hand, waiting for the booklet—"is finding out what you're reporting on for your research essay due tomorrow."

Mace drew a blank. "Um," he said, stalling. *TOMORROW?*

We still have assignments due? Wasn't the last week of school supposed to be for in-class pizza parties and movies and yearbook signings?

Seventh grade had been a year-long disappointment. He'd skated through, bored out of his wits. Why should it end any better? But he turned defeat into victory. "Funny you should ask," he said, completing the handoff to the teacher. "I'm doing a report on TURBO racing."

A scowl gathered on Mrs. Arbuckle's face. "Carson already took that subject."

Mace deflated, glancing at Carson. There he was, decked out in one of his rotating Gauntlet League TURBO jerseys. Today was maroon-and-gold day—*Pitchfork*'s colors, piloted by Australian Taz Nazaryan.

"And I actually go to races," Carson scoffed under his breath.

"No, Mrs. A.," Mace scrambled, pretending not to hear Carson. "I meant . . . I wanted to report on the *early days* of TURBO."

"Oh." Mrs. Arbuckle studied the brochure. "What do you mean?"

"You know"—Mace thought quickly—"how it all started as a result of the Space Race? Back in the 1960s, when

President Kennedy was paralyzed during that assassination attempt? The country started spending ten times more money on science and technology, and doctors healed his broken spine, and—"

"Save it for the report, Mace." The teacher handed the brochure back to him. "I suppose that's different enough. Go ahead."

"I was hoping for an extension." Mace wasn't lying. He was just being a little . . . artful . . . with the truth. "Time for a bit of—um, hands-on research?"

"Hands-on?"

"Yeah, like, no internet?" Mace explained.

"I like that idea," Mrs. Arbuckle said. She screwed up her face, deep in thought. "Actually, everyone gets an extra few days to turn in their essay. It'll be due Friday now. But that's the last day, so no late assignments."

The class cheered. Mace fielded a high five from Emily Turnbull in the next row.

"BUT," the teacher continued, *"All of you* need to provide a source that doesn't come from online."

"Not online? I don't get it," said a kid in the back, panic rising in her voice. "What does that even *mean*?"

Mrs. Arbuckle beamed with delight. “Go and interview somebody. Visit the place or historical site you’re reporting on. Log off. Be creative.”

“Give me back my high five,” grumbled Emily.

Carson whispered into Mace’s ear, “I’m changing my topic. Gonna do some hands-on research of TURBO wannabes. I’ll interview you, after school, with my fists.”

“Fists? Oh! Using sign language?” Mace fired back, sounding skeptical. “Okay. You’re on. I’ll meet you behind the cafeteria. Can’t wait to see how fluent you’ve gotten.”

The Gerb fumed. Whatever. Mace had no intention of tangling with Carson and his goons. He liked his nose just as it was, thank you very much. Besides, he was already booked this afternoon. He had a date with a legend: the *Event Horizon*!

////// CHAPTER TWO

Mountain Secondary School was perched on the slopes of Boulder, Colorado, nestled in an evergreen grove that stretched down from the foothills of the Rockies. It was the end of May, but a few patches of snow, dumped during a late spring superstorm, remained in the shadows of the lodgepole pines.

The metal shop was across the open-air quad. During passing time, Mace broke away from his classmates and wound around shaded snowbanks to the bike racks.

While the other students were cutting sheet metal into

garden ornaments, Mr. Hernandez often let Mace work on real problems: repairing the lawn mowers, upgrading sprinkler rotators, replacing engine parts for school vehicles. He got a kick out of upgrading whatever he was working on with refurbished aircraft components—his dad sometimes brought home interesting metal scraps from his airport job.

He took his bike lock and held it tight, closing his eyes. The bike's lightweight frame was custom modified from Goodwin-McCall twin-engine A-9 exhaust-port couplings. It had the gears and braking system of a downhill racer, with an XC dual-suspension fork and rear. Built piece by piece from airport scraps, because his parents could never afford to get him a brand-new bike. It was crazy cool. Better than anything you could buy. People were always eyeballing it. So, as a measure of extra security, Mace had sandpapered the digits off the bike-lock's dial. He didn't need to see the numbers. Mace could *feel* the combination.

Click. Tap. Clack. The lock opened in his hands. Mace pulled his bike free from the jumble and propped it against the machine shop's back door before looping around to the front to enter class with the other students. Mr. Hernandez stopped him as he arrived. "I have a lesson planned for the others, but you know it already. Can you finish threading that valve for the boiler system instead?"

Mace suppressed a grin. He'd been expecting this. "Be happy to, Mr. H."

His classmates watched him leave. He caught sight of the Gerb, who mouthed at him through an evil grin: "See you after class."

As soon as he was out of sight, Mace turned the corner and darted to the shop's back door to retrieve his bike. He eyed the canister of shielding gas over by the welder, a mixture of argon and carbon dioxide, and Mace knew immediately how he was going to mount it above his back wheel, creating a homemade rocket booster.

I'm not stealing this, he convinced himself. *It's a library check-out. And I need it.*

He jumped into action. He turned on the pipe threader, a machine loud enough to cover the tinkering he was about to begin.

First, he locked the aluminum canister of argon-carbon dioxide into place horizontally atop the back tire guard. Then he built a makeshift hammering pin, cocked and spring-loaded, and mounted it at the canister's neck. He ran a taut wire along the bike's cross tube up to the handlebar.

Mace inspected his creation and smiled mischievously. If only he had a couple of auxiliary TURBO transformer modules—he could give his getaway bike wings and fly away from school. That would really give them something to talk about.

"The crowds are going wild!" he said, mimicking the voice of TURBO race announcer Jax Anders. His daydream took hold, the pipe threader serving as crowd roar. "Blazer bags another win on the road to the Golden Glove!"

He'd seen plenty of televised races, but Mace had only been to one live TURBO event. That was in Denver two years ago. A Gauntlet Prix qualifier, part of the lead-up to the sport's epic championship sprint. His parents had taken him for his birthday. Mace appreciated it. He knew the tickets hadn't been cheap. Still, he'd been frustrated that their view had been obscured by the blimps hosting high-dollar spectators—like Carson Gerber and his family.

His mother had sensed his disappointment. "Enjoy what you have, Mace," she'd told him. "That's the key to happiness in life."

Mace disagreed. He thought the key to happiness was taking what you could, whenever you could get your hands on it. But once he'd settled in, Mace had to admit that it was a great day. It was amazing to see in person the blur of the vehicles as they entered the knot of stadium track in roadster form, roaring over the asphalt in front of the grandstands, and to hear the sound the water made as submersibles dove beneath the surface. Sure, he would have loved to be part of the underwater audience, who got to watch the race through special watertight viewports. But even now, years later, all Mace had to do was close his eyes to feel the roar of rocket engines as the submersibles morphed into jet mode and shot airborne.

Each passing aircraft had slapped Mace with a gust of wind. His parents had smiled along with him, hands to their chests, showing they understood the power of those machines.

He laughed remembering how his father had gotten angry with him for ruining their bucket of popcorn by diving a greasy hand into it. Mace hadn't even noticed how gross his hands were. He hadn't realized he'd been touching everything on their way into the stadium, which had funneled through an exhibition hall.

Mace hadn't been able to resist picking up every tool, feeling every display tire.

As he heard the students file back to their workbenches, Mace threw a greasy shop cloth over his new invention and began repairing the boiler valve.

Mace shut off the pipe threader, and when he strode back to the metal shop, it felt almost too quiet.

"You know," Mr. Hernandez whispered to him after pacing the room to inspect everyone's progress, "not much of a looker, but that's a sweet ride you have there. You could make those for a living. Good money in bikes."

Mace bit his tongue before saying what he really thought: *There's better money in TURBO racing.*

The bell rang. Everyone scurried outside. Mace half ran toward the main gate.

As he got to the edge of the parking lot, Carson emerged from the trees, gripping his handlebars. Two of his buddies flanked him. "I knew you'd skip our interview appointment." They dropped their bikes and circled in on Mace. "Don't even think about wiggling out here," Carson warned.

Three on one. Hmm. "Oh, I'm way past thinking about it."

Mace pushed his bike forward and leaped onto the seat. One of the boys swiped at him but missed. Mace pierced through the blockade as the others closed in. He turned onto the dirt path leading into the forest.

"Get him!" Carson yelled, but too late.

Mace was already gathering speed.

CHAPTER THREE //////

A hiking path wove through the dense lodgepole pines. Mace stuck to it, leaning in to each turn, staying off his brakes as much as possible.

"Move!" he shouted at two girls building a sad little snowman along the trail. They dove out of the way just as Mace sailed by.

He came to a meadow and spared a quick glance behind him. The Gerb and his minions were still on his tail, just entering the edge of the clearing.

Though they were pretty far back, Mace knew from

watching TURBO races that no lead could ever be taken for granted.

He gritted his teeth as he entered a heavy canopy of pine branches, dodging jagged tree roots and plowing through patches of snow. The terrain grew steep and treacherous, but he had no choice. He couldn't slow down. The Gerb was within taunting distance—and closing. "You're toast!"

You're probably right, Mace thought, and then the slope before him dove dramatically. He launched off the hillside and into the air.

He imagined he was piloting a TURBO trimorpher into the sky. He wished for wings, but . . .

. . . instead he landed hard, wheels pounding, teeth rattling, skidding to avoid a sharp-faced granite outcropping. He nearly lost control. But he didn't! He rumbled over a softer bed of fallen pine needles.

Time for the rocket booster?

He shot a look over his shoulder. Carson had chosen to navigate the boulder slope cautiously. The yellow-haired kid behind Carson had been more daring and wound up pitching forward. He sailed off his bike, landing with a thud among the graying snow banks. Mace pulled his eyes away.

His pain, my gain. He didn't need the booster now, not yet.

He descended through the pines toward Boulder. The lodgepoles gave way to fatter ponderosas and leafless oaks. A trunk came at him like a blur. He nearly collided with it, but swerved in the nick of time.

The hillside leveled off. Streets were visible through the evergreens. A city park opened up. *Like a TURBO terrain transition,* Mace thought. *Air-to-ground. Make every morph matter.* He broke through the trees and swerved through a playground, dodging toddlers and their protesting mothers, and hopped a curb.

"Watch it, hotshot!" one mom barked. "Other people live here, too!"

Don't mind me, Mace thought. *I'm just passing through. Fast.*

Carson and his remaining henchman emerged from the park. Like a cave bat, Mace didn't need to see them. He could hear the pulse of them, *feel* their presence. He knew they were closing in fast. Mace stood on his pedals and gave it all he had.

He saw a tall building with a red, tiled roof up ahead. The

city's urban trail system ended at the edge of the university campus. Home of the Colorado Museum of Aeronautics and Aerospace Engineering—and a perfect place to disappear into a crowd.

Mace gunned it across the quad, through a maze of buildings, toward the nearest bike path.

He knew Carson was hot on his tail. Mace veered to miss two lovebirds holding hands. The Gerb came around a corner from an unknown shortcut and caught up to him, clipping his back tire, forcing Mace to wobble and then dodge a skate rat who was somehow boarding while texting.

Now or never, he thought, and punched the makeshift lever on his handlebars.

The hammer fired against the nozzle of the gas canister, popping open the valve. A sickening swell of inertia yanked at Mace's gut. He accelerated faster than he'd expected—it felt awesome. He let out a "whoop" without even meaning to.

His pursuers fell behind. Mace's chest filled with relief as he snuck a peek over his shoulder and realized he could barely see them anymore.

It worked! I won!

Mace squeezed the brakes, once and then again. But he

didn't slow down! The booster was just too powerful.

It was then he realized: he'd forgotten an *off* switch.

The path ended up ahead at the foot of a building. He swerved onto the grass. His trajectory took him careening through hedges. There was no stopping. He screamed as he slammed into a chain-link fence at full speed.

The links caught his force and then sprang, flinging him backward on to the ground.

His lungs were flat. He gaped like a landlocked fish. Carson was on top of him before he could catch his breath. Mace tried desperately to wiggle free and escape, but the Gerb grabbed hold of Mace's shirt and twisted the collar into handles. "Sweet-talk your way out of this one," he growled. He pulled Mace off the ground and then slammed him down. The back of Mace's head smacked the earth.

A sickening ringing came to his ears, and then—nothing. Silence. All the sounds of the world were gone. He yelled but couldn't hear his own voice.

Deafness. A wave of panic overtook him.

He thrashed wildly, finally bucking Carson off. His attacker stood and stepped away, leaving Mace keeled over and panting.

His hearing came back to him. He snapped his fingers in front of his ears to confirm it and released a sob of relief. "Leave me alone!" he growled at Carson, who had taken another step back in confusion. "Just leave me alone, will you?"

The Gerb brushed grass clippings off his sleeves. "Why are you always so weird?"

Mace coughed and grimaced. The pain in his head grew from the back forward. He had slammed his cheeks and nose into that fence awfully hard. He tried to hold Carson's stare, but he had to look away to hold back the tears.

At least he could hear. The Gerb grabbed his bike and sped away, hooting and hollering.

Mace sat up and hugged his knees against the fence, staring at his Frankenstein bike. So much for his clever mods. And world's number-one TURBOnaut? Yeah, right.

Two bent rims. One flat tire. Handlebars pretzel-shaped. A perfect metaphor for his Frankenstein life.

CHAPTER FOUR //////

He might have sat there all afternoon, growing more and more depressed, except that the building in front of him finally caught his attention. A sign on the lawn read:

College of Engineering and Applied Science
Home of the Colorado Museum of Aeronautics
and Aerospace Engineering

Mace looked up and saw giant banners running down either side of the main entrance. The old-school *Event*

Horizon was pictured below a headline that read, *The History of TURBO Racing.*

I made it! Mace rose, rubbing his hip to push away the pain.

He locked his busted bike to the nearby rack and took the steps two at a time. He followed the TURBO banners through the corridors, past occasional college students. He stopped for a minute to gaze at a glass case displaying an early NASA spacesuit worn by a Boulder graduate. He paused to skim the graduate poster presentations—biotechnology advancements, nanotech research, materials science breakthroughs . . .

College looked awesome. But . . . universities were expensive. He knew his parents didn't have that kind of money. They worked four jobs between them, just to pay rent. He'd only get to college with scholarships, and that's why he'd be spending his summer in a mechanical engineering camp put on by the U. While the Gerb traveled the world, he would be here, building battle bots and model rockets.

He put his hands in the pockets of his grass-stained hoodie. Heavy feet carried him forward through the labyrinth of hallways.

When he finally arrived at the lobby to the exhibition hall, his spirits rose. An early-model rocket booster, polished and gleaming, hung suspended by cables from the dome ceiling, dangling over the admission desk. Mace felt a smile cross his face.

Look at those external nozzle flaps! How many blades per turbine? And the vanes . . . looks like an early Morton-Brown T4 series. Carbon polymer, or alloy?

"Welcome!" a large poster read. "On tour: get up close with a legendary early TURBO craft." A grainy photograph dominated the lower half of the sign: President Martin Luther King Jr. standing in front of *Event Horizon* following one of its numerous victories in the first year that TURBO racing officially became a sport. The president was shaking hands with its pilot, Quasar, whose mysterious identity remained hidden behind a black visor and all-black flight suit.

Mace approached the young woman behind the desk. "Hi. Can I get a ticket, please?" He slapped his school ID badge on the counter.

She looked up from a book, startled. "Ticket for what?" she said.

"The *Event Horizon* exhibit."

"Oh," she said, shaking her head. "No. That ended already, I'm afraid."

"What? Why?" Mace's hood fell back.

"Are you okay?" the girl asked, studying his face. "Were you in a fight?"

Mace ran a hand through his short, dark-brown hair. There was a natural part at the front of his scalp, and he had a permanent tuft of hair that stuck straight up over his forehead. It sprang back into place as his hand passed over it. Bits of grass rained down onto his shoulders. He pulled his hood back on. "There's no way I could get in and just take a quick peek?"

"Sorry—no. Owner wasn't happy with the turnout. Canceled in a hurry to get to a larger venue. Do you need some ice or something?" she asked, peering into his hood.

"Please . . . ," Mace begged, stuffing his hands into pockets to hide the fact that he was so upset he was starting to shake. "It's for a school assignment. I promise I'll be—"

"I would if I could, but the machine's already gone. Boxed up at the airport, ready to be shipped off to the next museum. You could go see it in Albuquerque this weekend."

"Albuquerque! That's—" Mace's hands balled into fists. He unclenched them. "Thank you anyway," he told the college girl.

"Sorry," she said. "Can I at least give you some ibuprofen? Your eye is swelling shut. It's gotta hurt. What's that cross pattern? You insult a waffle iron?"

"A chain-link fence," Mace admitted.

"Where are your parents?"

"At work." He sighed.

"Well, give me their numbers."

"I'm fine," Mace said.

"Listen, I need to call someone. You're a mess. It can either be your parents, or campus security. Up to you."

"I can take care of—" Mace paused, then ground his teeth. His bike had bent rims and a flat. He had no money for a bus. Walking home from here would take ages. He was stiff and miserable. He gave up and told the girl to text his mom.

"You don't have a phone?" she asked.

Only kid at school who still doesn't. Thanks for rubbing it in my face. He sighed and shook his head.

She picked up the phone at the desk and punched in numbers.

Mace rolled his eye that worked. He put his hand over hers. "I told you, you have to *text* her."

"Huh? I'm not supposed to use my personal phone at work."

Mace forced a smile. "Just—will you just text her, please? Or let me do it?" He wasn't in the mood to explain his reasoning to a stranger right now.

Her expression made it clear she thought he was being difficult, but she pulled a smartphone out of her pocket and slid it across the counter to him.

"Thanks," he replied.

A few minutes later he shuffled out to the curb to wait for his mom. She would come. She always did. But she'd be furious with him for costing her a half a day's pay.

As he sat next to his broken bike on the cold sidewalk, watching the sunset, he thought about *Event Horizon*. In real life, the term meant the line beyond which light can't escape a black hole. Figured. Like a law of physics, Mace was trapped on the ground, while the world of real TURBO racing happened beyond his reach.

CHAPTER FIVE /////

The car ride home was silent. A silence like peanut butter on the roof of Mace's mouth. Sticky. Uncomfortable. He put on the radio. His mother stared forward with her hands gripping the steering wheel. She wouldn't glance his way.

Was it just his imagination, or was her long black hair flecked with more gray than before? Sunspots speckled her temples, and short pale lines radiated out from the corners of her eyes. She was small and thin, almost delicate, but she had a hard set to her jaw that made her seem all the more intimidating when she was mad.

"Why are you getting into fights again?" She spoke the words aloud. She rarely used her voice. But she wouldn't look at him, so it was pointless for him to offer an answer.

They turned onto their street, dodging a mangy-looking cat that bounded beneath a rusty truck on cinder blocks. Mace stepped out of the car at their driveway to unlock and roll back the chain-link gate. His mom pulled forward, and Mace closed the gate.

She got out of the car, and Mace ran up behind her and tapped her shoulder. Finally, she gave him her eyes.

"I'm sorry," he signed.

"Fix your bike. Then go to your room," she signed in reply. The veins on the backs of her hands stood out strongly.

"I didn't start the fight," he signed.

"You never do," she answered, and marched into the house.

"But it's true," he complained out loud, but her back was already turned, so she couldn't read his lips.

In the garage, he banged his bike rims back into shape and patched his flat tire as night fell. When he finally came back into the house, he found an ice-bundled cloth waiting for him on the counter. He pressed it to his swollen eye. The house was silent. Mom was on the couch, staring at the TV with the sound off but the closed captioning scrolling. Mace touched her shoulder. She turned to look at him. He pointed at the cloth and signed, "Thank you."

"Are you okay?" she signed back.

He nodded.

Her lips grew straight and firm. She signed, letting her frustration show: "Clocking out early will make us tight on money this month. It's a big deal, M. It has to stop."

"I know. I'm sorry." His eyes smarted. He masked them with the ice wrap.

"We'll talk about it when your dad gets home."

Mace slouched to his room, kicked his legs up, and fell heavily onto his bed. He shifted the ice to the other eye.

How could he make them understand? Fights kept finding him, because . . . well, maybe he *was* at fault. This rivalry with the Gerb, for example, had started last year. Carson had been mocking a deaf person, waving his arms around and making noises. And without thinking, Mace had slugged him, giving *el Gerberino* a bruise that had lasted a week. Mace had avoided suspension by offering to work in the mechanic's shop on school vehicles. He was already doing that anyway, but the principal hadn't known about it.

Mace listened for his father's car. The neighbor's dog was barking. Other than that . . . nothing. Even Mom's television show was silent. To Mace's trained ears, silences were different from one another. This one was thick, chunky, like milk that had been left on the counter too long.

How could he have missed an up-close encounter with a TURBO craft? *Event Horizon* had been in town all week! Free admission! But he'd missed out. And he still had to write a report on it. Typical.

The report! He better get started on it.

Mace fired up his old desktop computer, typed "Event Horizon TURBO" into the search bar, and lost himself in watching archive footage of the first-gen trimorpher.

It went seamlessly from ground to water to air, the exhaust ports flapping open and closed as it throttled up and then throttled down. The wings cut the air so that vapor streamed off the tips of the fins. When Mace looked close enough, he could see that there was a pulse to the vehicle. Like a heartbeat. It rippled along the hull.

The other vehicles didn't display the same . . . poetry of

movement. *Sabrewing, Navigator, Patriot*—that year's top finishers—showed no hint of similar . . . grace.

Event Horizon and her masked pilot had almost won the first Gauntlet Prix. But a crash had ended their bid for the Glove. The pilot, Quasar, whose true identity had never been revealed, had vanished after that fateful accident.

Mace watched the crash from several available angles. Quasar had built a comfortable lead but had braked sharply coming into the final stretch. *Sabrewing* almost smashed into *Event Horizon* but veered at the last second, clipping *Event Horizon*'s wheels. There was a flash at that moment, washing out all camera angles. Probably an exploding coupler. Quasar lost control, snagged on the road shoulder. The vehicle flipped, hitting the track's concrete safety barrier.

The explosion had been massive.

Why had Quasar braked when there was no need?

Mace searched to learn more about the masked 'Naut in Black. Conspiracy theories were all over the map, with evidence pointing everywhere. Some believed the TURBO Association had covered up Quasar's death. Some believed the pilot remained in a coma to this day. One site swore Quasar was now a pig farmer in Iowa. Mace couldn't begin to guess which theories were true.

He began to write his report, citing facts from memory.

> The sport of TURBO racing is undoubtedly the most popular racing sport in the world today. But this wasn't always true. TURBO racing has come a long way since the early days when pioneering engineers worked in strict secrecy to develop transforming vehicles for a wide variety of military purposes.

Mace stopped typing. He couldn't concentrate. That pulse—the "breathing" of the *Event Horizon*. Mace couldn't shake it. He tapped the rhythm on the desk, imagining tighter corners on all three terrains. He could shave off *seconds* of track time by nailing that beat.

He returned to studying film clips. They were decades old, but *Event Horizon* performed almost like a present-day trimorpher. It was *waaay* ahead of the competition. It wasn't even close. Until it flamed out in the Prix, racing *Event Horizon* was like pitting a brand-new Ferrari against Model T Fords. *Event Horizon* had won every race it entered.

Still, even today's trimorphers didn't breathe the way *Event Horizon* had.

Mace caught himself whispering instructions aloud as he watched old footage. "No. You should have waited another half second there. . . . Pull up, pull up. . . . You should have passed him on the left that time.

"I could win with that machine," he told the air.

The simulator at the mall offered a near-real piloting experience. Mace knew where every button and switch was. He'd risen in the global leaderboards with each virtual run. But his body knew the pod's movements were fake. If he could slip into a real trimorpher, feel the road, the water, the air—he knew his times would be even better. Watching vids of a pilot who wasn't taking maximum advantage of *Event Horizon*'s full power was driving him nuts.

He couldn't shake the thought that if he had been driving her in that fateful Prix, he would've won.

////////////////////////

"When are you going to realize that your choices affect others?"

Here it was. The Lecture. Mace had known it was coming. He'd heard it before. His father signed with intensity. His fingers were blunt-nailed and rough with old scars.

Dad had just gotten home from his day shift at the bottling plant, where he worked the assembly line. His beige, button-up uniform had sticky stains all over the chest. Mace guessed a bottle of soda had exploded on him again.

Dad sat forward at the dinner table, arms crossed over his growing paunch. His gray hair was cut short, and a five-o'clock shadow crept down his thick neck. He had been Deaf since birth, and unlike Mace's mom, who'd lost her hearing when she was six, he had never learned to speak and so never tried.

Mom sat at the table with them, nodding along.

"I'm sorry," Mace told them, "but I went to the TURBO exhibit for a *homework* assignment. Not to pick a fight. Those boys would have attacked me anywhere."

"Why?" Mom asked. "Was it Mr. Gerber's son? Should I complain again?"

"No!" Mace blurted. "No. It wasn't—I can take care of myself."

"By stealing a welding canister to make your bike race faster?" Dad signed.

This caught Mace by surprise. "How'd you know that?" he asked.

"I've got two eyes, don't I?" Mom signed. "I saw your bike."

Mace hated that she had figured that out. "It's the end of the school year. I'm just borrowing it," he tried.

"I'm not interested in your excuses, Mace. What if Mr. H. needs that over the summer? You only think about yourself. And the rest of us pick up the pieces. I have to pull a double shift tonight to cover for Mom's lost hours," Dad told him. "No allowance this week. No mall."

Mace finished his food without looking up. No mall would mean losing his number-one slot on the simulator rankings again. He stood in a huff and marched to his room. He could still sneak to the mall, he figured. And he knew where his parents kept their change in their bedroom closet.

He wouldn't swipe much money. Just enough to stay on the leaderboard.

On his computer screen was a repeating GIF of *Event Horizon* cruising to an easy win at the Tokyo 200. That pulse. Mace could almost feel it.

His unfinished report gnawed at him. He sat down to continue writing.

But something else gnawed at him more.

Event Horizon—it breathed. Like a racehorse, it knew

how to win. Quasar was just a jockey.

Mace was a better jockey.

He shut the computer down. It was late, and he still had a few days to finish his work.

He couldn't shake the thought. He wanted to see it for himself, *feel* if he was right. But *Event Horizon* was at the airport, about to be shipped to Albuquerque.

At the airport . . . he thought. And then he remembered Dad signing, *I have to pull a double shift tonight* . . .

It was a long shot, but what if *Event Horizon* wasn't in Albuquerque yet? What if it was still in town—at the airport?

Where his dad worked.

CHAPTER SIX /////

Sneaking out of the house past Deaf parents was more of a ninja move than one might think. Mom and Dad had a sixth sense when it came to Mace. The softest vibration would wake them. But Mace had learned the hard way which routes to take, and he congratulated himself as he wiggled beneath a blanket in the back of his dad's sedan unnoticed. All he had to do now was wait for Dad to come out and then remain stock-still until they were inside the airport.

He fell asleep waiting, and his eyes startled open when the car rocked and the driver's-side door slammed shut. The engine churned, gasped, tried to turn over, and died. It had always been cranky in the cold. Dad tried the ignition again, pumping the gas furiously, and finally the car started with a backfire. Mace risked a glance up front as they reversed out of the driveway. His father was bundled up in his overalls and a thick jacket. His breath plumed in the cold, like smoke.

At the curb, Dad got out to close the gate, and Mace shifted his weight, looking for a comfortable position. *There's no turning back now,* he realized with a terrified thrill.

Twenty minutes later, the car slowed to a stop, and his dad rolled down his window. *We're here!* Mace's heart was in his throat. He held his breath as his dad flashed his security credentials to the gatehouse guard, then pulled forward and around the corner into his spot. With jarring speed, Dad was out of the car and gone.

And like that, Mace was alone. He knew this was a bad idea. He shouldn't have come, and yet . . . *Event Horizon* might very well be sitting nearby. A private viewing all his own.

Sliding soundlessly out the back door, Mace stuck to the shadows and stayed low as he snuck away from the employee parking lot and onto the airport's high-security tarmac. He hustled over to an idling fuel truck and scanned for any sign he'd been spotted. The airport was quiet enough that it felt abandoned.

"Don't be fooled," he whispered to himself. "They're out there." He was referring, of course, to the guards. And the dogs. And the security cameras. And the all-seeing control tower. And anyone waiting for a flight. All they'd have to do is peer out the terminal windows to catch a glimpse of a twelve-year-old cat burglar.

Patches of darkness between cones of lamplight formed his surest path to the hangars across the runway, where Mace assumed an invaluable TURBO racer like *Event Horizon* would be kept. He checked again to make sure the coast was clear and made a run for it. The rushing midnight air came in hard off the lake at the runway's far end. Mace slipped behind a parked plane to catch his breath. He strained to hear whether anyone had spotted him and was moving his way, but all he could detect was his own thundering heartbeat. He darted off again, not daring to come out of his crouch.

Nearly at the first hangar, his ears caught the roar of a plane coming in to land. The runway. He realized he'd sprinted out into the middle of the *runway.*

This was an airport after all. He had forgotten to factor in landing *planes*!

The ground rumbled. Mace threw himself into a dive-roll as the plane's wheels touched down. He brushed the dirt from his pant legs as he watched a small ground crew hustle over to taxi the plane onto the airport apron. Mace sprinted quick as he could toward the hangar.

A security officer came around the corner, walkie-talkie in hand. Mace plastered himself up against the dark side of the hangar and held his breath. The officer gazed out at the runway and spoke into his radio. "Must'a been an animal."

"I don't know," came the reply. "Pilot seemed pretty certain it was big and on two legs."

The guard mumbled a reply and headed back to his normal rounds. Mace slid his back along the hangar wall until he came to a door. The handle turned, but the door was latched along an iron plate with a thick combination padlock.

Mace grinned. He rested the lock in his hand, allowed its weight to nest into his palm. He closed his eyes and turned the combination dial. Somewhere inside the padlock's belly, a tiny pin slipped into a groove.

To Mace, it felt like a sledgehammer dropping. One hundred notches to choose from, but he felt the next pin jerk when he spun it back to the right spot, as if it called out to him: *stop here.* Mace yanked on the lock. The door swung open with a faint creak.

He passed through a hallway to a vast warehouse interior. He set his jaw stubbornly and kept going until he caught sight of a vaguely disc-shaped mass, covered with cloth, alone in the middle of the warehouse, where the red light of the Exit sign was dimmest.

He stepped forward and touched the cloth, running a trembling hand along its shape. He could feel the cloaked object shudder a little under his touch.

What he had guessed from the videos—he could now feel in person: a pulse. It was like a hibernating grizzly bear. He knew he was detecting one of its many pumps, probably circulating antifreeze through the machine's veins—but still. *She's alive, all right.*

Mace walked around the beast, touching the covered hull, running his fingertips over what he was sure was her glass canopy. He turned and retraced his steps, his opposite hand now in the lead.

This had to be it. He curled his fingers into the cloth and wrenched it backward.

Event Horizon.

It was on a mount in aircraft form, its wings half-extended—tucked back but at the ready. The pale-red light reflected off her flawless black surface. The engine rose torpedo-shaped beneath the dorsal fin. The nose narrowed to needle sharpness.

He laid both hands flat on the top of the craft, just below the tear-shaped glass hatch. Detecting a hair's-width seam, he ran his finger along it and stumbled upon a delicate latch. The canopy hissed open, and panels inside awoke with faint lighting.

Heart thudding, he leaned forward and peered inside. The ejector seat beckoned him. He glanced around the dark room. "Research," he said aloud. "My teacher told me to do this." His words echoed. The hangar was so quiet. A silence of permission.

He dragged over a wooden crate and used it to climb inside.

"Oh, man." He whistled.

Event Horizon's interior was *exactly* the same as the

simulator pod at the mall. *Cool.* He felt at home. Every surface was covered in buttons and switches, controls and panels, displays and lighting. He simply couldn't resist. He ran his fingers along the interfaces, felt something deeper—that clicking pump—but also an internal hum. A pulse.

This was no fancy video game. This was real.

He felt like the controls were an extension of his own body. He allowed himself to imagine it: Mace Blazer, TURBOnaut of *Event Horizon.* He laughed at the thought. If only . . .

A dark display screen lit, reading:

FINGERPRINTS VERIFIED

WEIGHT/HEIGHT PARAMETERS CONFIRMED

The cockpit hatch closed. Mace laughed nervously, then realized his danger with a sudden jolt. He clocked his head on the glass above him. As he fell back down, the seat softened, enveloping him, then hardened again. Smart foam. His arms were free but otherwise he was immobilized.

Mace was trapped.

"Hey!" he yelled, to no one in particular. "Let me out of here! I'm sorry! I—"

Text appeared on the display screen.

WELCOME MBLAZE07

AUTHORIZATION GRANTED

He gaped, dumbfounded. A single laugh coughed out of him. "What the—?!"

The humming he'd only barely detected was now everywhere—and loud—even through the headrest wrapped snugly around his ears. The beast had awoken. "No. No," Mace said. His heart was in his throat. "Don't do that."

INITIALIZING

Event Horizon lowered. He heard the wooden crate crush into splinters. The exterior shell folded and shifted around him, revealing tires, a fatter nose. The wings disappeared. When the craft touched the ground, Mace was behind the wheel of a roadster.

The hangar bay door opened. Blue-and-red flashing lights flooded the warehouse interior. A cold, terrified yelp of alarm escaped his lips.

Cops were everywhere. "Get out of the . . . vehicle . . . with your hands up!" demanded a man with a bullhorn.

"I can't!" Mace screamed. "I don't know what—" He fell silent, realizing they'd never hear—and that he was in major trouble. He'd broken into an airport. He'd nearly caused a landing plane to crash. He looked like he was stealing a freakin' TURBO craft. "I'm going to jail for the rest of my life," he said aloud, and knew it was true.

The steering mechanism rose and extended toward Mace's hands. The display suddenly flashed:

YOU'RE NOT GOING TO JAIL TODAY

He released a bark of laughter. "Is this for real? Who is this?" he asked the screen.

DRIVE

Mace could feel pedals rise to meet his feet. The engines revved, the reverberation hummed throughout the whole craft and up through Mace's spine. His eyes widened. His heart pounded.

The police officers were arriving in twos and fours. Flashing lights rushed in from the direction of the airport runway. The screen glowered at him:

DRIVE

Mace shook his head. "No. There's a mistake. I can't—who are you?" he asked again. He was certain this wasn't AI. *Event Horizon* itself had no artificial intelligence. *Someone* was talking to him.

DON'T WORRY ABOUT THAT NOW

A SWAT van fishtailed to a stop. Its back doors sprang open. Officers emerged and fanned out along the tarmac in a large arc. Mace groaned. They wore heavy armor and carried what looked like machine guns, pointed downward but at the ready.

YOU BETTER GO BEFORE THEY BLOW THE TIRES

"Uh. But . . . where?" Mace laughed.

I'LL TELL YOU WHERE TO GO

This was *so* not a good idea, but he couldn't see another choice. If he got caught, he'd go to jail. And he realized aloud with a flash of dread: *"Dad will lose his job."*

Mace gripped the wheel. He exhaled a long breath—and stomped the gas.

The tires squealed. He lurched forward. The force of acceleration pushed him deep into the smart cushioning.

The police scattered.

CHAPTER SEVEN //////

Mace was surprised by how light a touch the fuel pedal needed.

He clutched the wheel and wove through the blockade of police cruisers. The light panels were blaring with proximity alerts. But Mace tuned it all out. He didn't need a flashing light to tell him he was driving dangerously. He knew somehow he'd be fine if he just focused on what he could detect with his own senses. He felt out a path through the blockade. The steering was hair-trigger sensitive. The tires gripped the blacktop like glue. Mace felt the engines hum. He screamed, terrified . . . and blindingly happy.

He shifted, cut through a line of parked airplanes toward open tarmac. When he felt he'd earned enough distance, he hit the brakes a bit too hard. The sudden stop was rough on his stomach, but the smart foam grabbed him and absorbed his body's lost inertia.

WHY ARE YOU STOPPING?

"Just—give me a second. I just broke about a dozen laws and plowed through a police force, okay?"

YOU STIRRED UP A HORNET'S NEST

IT'S TIME TO SCRAM!

Red-and-blue lights grew brighter from behind.

He eyed the obvious exits and saw that he was surrounded by police. Vans were double- and triple-parked in front of gates. One gate was suspiciously unprotected and Mace glimpsed spikes glinting in the moonlight. They were trying to lure him into a trap.

His heart jackhammered. "So, how the heck am I getting out of here?"

LET'S SEE WHAT YOU'VE GOT

"What does that mean? Is this some sort of insane test?"

There was no answer.

"Tell me where I need to go, at least!"

START WITH DENVER

"Denver! That's more than forty miles away!"

The screen paused, blank for several beats, then flashed.

YOU DO REALIZE WHAT YOU'RE PILOTING, DON'T YOU?

The comment snapped something loose within Mace. Call it reality.

I'm piloting a TURBO racer.

Mace peered down the long taxiway at the running blue landing lights that seemed to converge in the distance. The sky was the limit.

Literally.

"You want Denver? I'll give you Denver," he said, slamming his foot down on the pedal. He couldn't help but shriek as he whipped through each gear and shot through a hole in the tightening net of security vehicles.

The pulse. *Remember how this thing breathes. You're just a jockey. Let her do the work.* He shifted, gave a half count, shifted again. A laugh extended into a yell. Mace hovered his hand over the light display. The fence beyond the end of the runway was growing large. The icon he was readying to punch said *Air Morph*.

WHOA, TEX, MAYBE GET A FEEL FOR THE GROUND FIRST

"Why? This *is* a runway, isn't it?"

THERE'S NO AUTOPILOT

YOU MIGHT WANT TO EASE INTO HER

There was a reservoir beyond the airport. His blood was pumping as he stared out at the water. He could read a sign in the bright headlights: Hayden Lake. Beyond that, the darkness of the Rocky Mountains, capped with silvery hoods of snow.

Lake, thought Mace. "Hey, helper person," he said. "How long does it take *Event Horizon* to morph from ground to air and then from air to water?"

EACH MORPH TAKES EXACTLY 1.64 SECONDS

Mace neared the end of the runway. An airplane flew overhead, rising, aborting its landing. "And how much time is needed *between* morphs?" he asked.

NO ONE HAS EVER TRIED

BACK-TO-BACK MORPHS BEFORE

"Oh, great," Mace said. "Well, there's a first for everything." He popped the clutch into high gear and slammed the morph-to-air sequencer. Mace held his breath as the jet engines growled awake. *Event Horizon* picked up speed, sprouted wings, caught lift, and retracted its wheels into its underbelly—all within seconds.

With a sickening pull at his gut, Mace was suddenly air-borne, sailing over the airport fence and blowing the Hayden Lake sign out of the ground. Mace felt more power stirring behind him than he could have imagined. He pounded the light display again, trusting the machine to respond before he flew into the side of the mountains.

WAIT! WHAT ARE YOU DOING?

The wings retracted. The wheels remained tucked. The afterburner snapped off as quickly as it had fired up. A turbine began to churn. Mace dropped from the sky like a bomb . . .

. . . and pierced the dark surface of the lake.

Make every morph—!

He struck bottom.

Matter.

The smart foam already gripped his body tightly, but nothing could save him from the shock of such a quick stop. He gaped for breath with flattened lungs.

Too shallow! He should have known better. This was a reservoir, for crying out loud, not the ocean.

He heard an ominous crack. The cockpit began to fill with icy black water.

Mace gulped back a scream.

Within seconds, the water was up to his waist. He couldn't believe how cold it was! He thrashed but the smart cushioning only tightened its grip. He needed to get out of here! He was going to drown! "What do I do? I need to eject!"

DIAGNOSTICS ARE FINE

YOU JUST NEED TO PRESSURIZE THE CABIN

THE CRAFT DIDN'T HAVE TIME TO SEAL

"But I heard a crack." Mace was frantic now. The frigid water was closing around his neck. It was so cold. He couldn't draw in a proper breath.

PRESSURIZATION WILL TAKE CARE OF IT

PUSH THE GREEN ICON NEXT TO YOUR RIGHT ELBOW

Problem was, Mace couldn't see anything below the surface of the rising water. It was black as tar down there.

He took in as much air into his lungs as he could and stuck his head underwater. He could see the dim glow of lights along the lower control panels. Panicky and terrified, he cast around for something green by his right elbow. *There*. He saw it! But he was still immobilized by his seat. His left arm couldn't reach that far. He craned his right arm around, instead, twisting his wrist, and glanced the glowing icon.

Jets of air roiled through the cabin. The water level lowered. He let out his pent-up breath, and within seconds, the cabin was bone-dry and he was being blasted with warm air from the vents.

He laughed but couldn't control his nervous shaking. That had been terrifying.

"All right. Let's get out of the water," he told himself.

He tried the steering wheel and the pedals. The craft sprang into forward motion, scraping at first along the bed of sediment below. The handling was just as tight and responsive as it was on land. Only difference was he could move up and down as well as from side to side. Mace noted that this was probably a good opportunity to get a feel for flying *Event Horizon*. As eager as he was to get back on land, he took an extra few moments to familiarize himself with the controls.

Advancing through murky blackness, he reached the far shore of the lake and found himself partially emerged. "Great," he realized. "I'm a beached whale."

He remembered TURBO races he'd watched. Submarine-to-ground morphs usually involved a ramp—and a fair amount of speed. The trimorpher needed momentum and a bit of lift to allow the wheels to lock into place.

"Let's try this again."

He reversed the turbines, backed into the water. When he punched forward this time, he gave it all he had.

Event Horizon shot up through the surface, ramping off a sandbar. Mace toggled the roadster. By the time the craft hit the ground, it was on wheels.

No red-and-blue flashing lights in front of him anymore. The proximity sensors were silent. That was an improvement. But the authorities would be arriving from the highway any second. He glimpsed a road sign indicating the way toward Denver. He took to the nearest pavement, whipped a fast left turn, and gunned it down the street to meet up with the highway leading into the city.

He didn't hold back, driving fast, faster, testing his own limits. The controls were intuitive, familiar, but he was still getting a feel for real-world handling. He took the curves with greater ease each time, zipped around other cars on the road, shot forward toward the city lights, the miles blending together.

He couldn't believe how quickly he reached the outskirts of Denver.

A strange throbbing met his ears. Mace cast his gaze

upward. A police helicopter had drawn even with him and was tracking his moves.

"Okay, friendly texting guy, I'm here. Denver's kind of big. Can you give me more specifics?"

A map materialized on one of the displays, showing his current location and providing a suggested route.

HEAD SOUTH THROUGH DOWNTOWN AND MERGE
ONTO I-25 TOWARD COLORADO SPRINGS

Really? Mace thought. The police were above him. He could go very fast, but he could never outrun a dispatcher who could radio ahead to new units.

The throbbing sensation doubled. Mace flicked his eyes upward again. A second chopper. This one read *News Channel 4*.

Oh, nice. The morning news. Should I wave to my parents?

The streets of Denver were quiet, but not empty. Mace dodged traffic. He saw a cluster of cop cars gathering far down the wide street. That was a mistake on their part. He executed a sharp left turn then jogged right again. Like a rabbit, he realized he needed to make his path random.

"This is a TURBO race," he told himself, unable to suppress a grin. "And I'm going to win it."

He made his way through downtown, artfully rerouting whenever the police tried to corner him, confounding the whirlybirds above as he entered the canyon streets towered by skyscrapers. He readied to execute a sharp turn, but instinct cautioned him. Continuing straight instead, he was able to confirm his suspicion: a wall of three cop cars approached at high speed along that avenue. The dashboard proximity alerts chimed.

He zigged onto Stout Street. Oncoming cruisers rushed forward to head him off. *Time to zag!* They closed in. He bolted the wrong way up Eighteenth, doubled back. The Ritz-Carlton lobby driveway caught his attention. *I'll spring my own trap,* he thought. He pulled up to the lobby doors, two cruisers tailing him, two cruisers coming at him. He peeled away, trapping all four cop cars in a nose-to-nose knot as he slipped between the oncomers. He was Pac-Man on a power pellet, the flashing blue ghosts his helpless foes. Finally, he gunned it down an empty stretch of Broadway and veered onto I-25.

His tires were balding; he could feel them slipping on the road surface. He remembered a Prix qualifier only two months ago, in which "Grizzly" Jack Adams went too many laps without changing tires—and ultimately slammed *Ursa Major* into a retaining wall while coming off a sharp bank in the track. "I better take a pit stop," he joked.

He gathered speed, shifting through gear after gear. "I'm free and—nope." There was a problem up ahead. A sea of red and blue clogged the way forward about a mile or so down the highway.

"Um, ideas?"

TIME TO GROW SOME WINGS

Yes. Mace exhaled. "I thought you'd never ask." He barreled toward the roadblock. Cop cars raced up the next on-ramp and flanked him. He remembered the staggering thrust he had felt upon fleeing the airport, knew to anticipate it this time.

He pounded the morph-to-air icon, felt the g-forces push his body back into his seat, felt that strange weightlessness that comes with leveling off, and like that, he was rocketing over the Denver skyline and waving the police goodbye.

But Mace wasn't in the clear yet. The displays lit up. A "rival craft" was riding his wake. He laughed. Apparently, *Event Horizon* wasn't programmed to distinguish police helicopters from trimorphers.

"RENEGADE CRAFT, YOU'RE NOT AUTHORIZED TO ENTER DENVER AIRSPACE," came an amplified cry from behind. The police. "LAND IMMEDIATELY OR WE'LL BE FORCED TO BRING YOU DOWN."

Mace nudged the throttle forward. The police chopper matched his speed.

"LAND NOW. OR YOU'LL BE DEEMED A CLEAR AND PRESENT DANGER TO THE STATE OF COLORADO AND BE SHOT DOWN."

Blown out of the sky? "Not cool!" Mace told the cockpit. "Help!"

The text reply was as concise as the plea had been.

GO FASTER

"You asked for it. Faster it is." Mace increased velocity. Red lights lit up the interior. Screens all over flashed:

PROJECTILE DETECTED

TAKE EVASIVE ACTION

This had never been part of the simulator.

Mace veered far to the left. He heard a crackle, felt a menacing reverberation, and saw the angry, precision flames of a missile glance off his hull.

"No more messing around." Mace punched the throttle

all the way forward. His speed seemed to double.

"CEASE AND DESIST!" The threat was quieter now.

He gave the lever another push, and the pulsating sensation of Denver PD's helicopter grew faint behind him.

The checkered flag was his.

He turned in wide arcs, danced, rolling into graceful flips, rising and falling swiftly just for the sweetly sick weight it put on his stomach.

Mace Blazer, TURBOnaut.

ALL RIGHT, RENEGADE,

FLY LOW TO STAY OFF RADAR

"Hey, I almost got blowed up. Let me celebrate, will ya?"

YOU'RE HEADING TO MONUMENT VALLEY IN ARIZONA

YOU'LL SEE BLUE LANDING STRIP LIGHTS LEADING STRAIGHT

TOWARD THE FORMATIONS

LAND AND DRIVE INTO THE ROCK

Mace read the message several times. Monument Valley was a day's drive away from Denver. A long day. But not today. Not in *Event Horizon*. Half an hour later he was over the stately rock formations and the wild, open expanse of the Arizona desert. A landing strip lined with flashing blue runway lights led dead into a rock wall.

An uncomfortable revelation came home to roost: *No autopilot.* "Oh. Um. I have to land this thing?" he asked. "For reals?"

A light display flickered to life against the front canopy window. Relief poured over Mace. Landings in the mall's simulator were second nature, and these new light dials and gauges felt familiar. He just had to keep his altitude, rate of descent, and alignment within the given margins. No sweat. He'd done it countless times before—and *most* of those times, he'd nailed the landing.

He made a few calculated adjustments to account for crosswinds and air density, and touched down as a roadster. "Like playing a concert violin . . ." He'd started to congratulate himself but the heavy landing blew out the baldest back tire. He bounced, rattling his teeth. The craft careened off-kilter. The rhythm was gone. The panel lights were freaking out. A towering rock face closed in at what felt like hundreds of miles an hour. He was sure he was about to die. Mace braced for impact, but the headlights caught the movement: a hole in the rock wall yawned open. In an instant, he found himself skidding down a long tunnel, slowing, twisting and turning. The vehicle felt like it was coming apart at the seams. He settled to a stop in the middle of a cavernous, empty garage.

The space looked rather similar to the hangar he'd originally broken out of—a mere forty minutes ago. His seat released him. The canopy opened. He stole a breath of air, half expecting to choke on poisonous Martian gasses.

Nothing happened.

He hoisted himself out, hopped onto the concrete, and waited as he heard the rock-wall entrance groan shut behind him.

Then, footsteps on concrete.

A slender figure just slightly taller than Mace appeared before him out of the dark, dressed in black.

"'Sup," tried Mace, extending a lonely hand. "Are you Friendly Texting Guy? Sorry about the tire. And, er, the shocks. And the belly. And the paint job." He winced.

"Welcome, Mace Blazer." The stranger's voice was muffled by the glass of a black helmet, polished and gleaming against the lights. Swirled grooves on the helmet formed an insignia that Mace recognized: a star being consumed by a void disk, with cones of X-ray radiation emanating from it.

Mace froze. Was it possible? Could this be *Event Horizon*'s TURBOnaut, who had vanished decades ago?

"Are you—" He gulped back the dryness in his throat. "Are you Quasar?"

The figure stiffened. "I haven't been called that in a long time."

"Awesome," Mace said, his voice echoing in the cold of the chamber. "Wait. How do you know my name?"

"I've been testing you all year, Mace."

"Me? Seriously?"

"Yes. Very seriously. Now welcome to your final exam."

CHAPTER EIGHT /////

"No way," Mace said. His addled brain was starting to put the pieces together. *Touch-screen displays . . . that's why my prints were on file. . . .*

The helmet nodded. "The simulator. You're one of the top players in the world, so of course I've had my eye on you. But anyone can excel at a game. I'm looking for those few who show true passion for the sport. *Event Horizon* has been on tour all year, nearly everywhere I've placed a simulator. The super fans always insist on sitting within the cockpit. Your prints activated her. And when you successfully started her up, that was your golden ticket for a chance to come to the chocolate factory."

Mace's mouth hung open. A response snagged somewhere in his throat, but never materialized. *Willy Wonka? Is that you?*

"You have a black eye," the muffled voice behind Quasar's visor said. "Should we test for concussion? Did you hit your head on your water entry?"

Mace didn't understand, then he remembered his fight with Carson. *That was today!* He shook his head. "Oh, no. It's nothing. That's from a whole 'nother . . . lifetime."

"Come with me," Quasar said, and marched down a hallway. Lights came on, revealing a long concrete corridor that descended into the mountain. But Mace stood frozen in place. He glanced around the hangar numbly, his eyes resting for a moment on the trimorpher he'd just *flown* here, on his own, with half a state hot on his tail.

Concussion. Yeah. "Carson rattled my brain loose, that's what happened," he told himself. "This is all a dream."

He pinched himself. "Ow!" he said.

He sprang after the masked figure. The hallway was

long. The lights clicked on as Mace approached and off after he passed beneath them. It made for an odd, slow-strobe-light-like sensation. Quasar did not slow down for him. "There's a lot of theories out there that you're dead, you know," he said, catching up to the pilot.

"Rumors," Quasar replied. "But still, for all intents and purposes, Quasar *is* dead. Better that way."

Mace didn't know what that meant, or how to respond. He had to trot to keep up. He thought of another explanation . . . a scarier one. This could be a trap. *But . . . why?*

"Let the record show I correctly guessed I'm being punked," he declared.

"Did you fly here tonight in a cardboard box?"

Quasar had a point. The escape from the airport had really happened. No way that could have been a stunt. He'd been in *Boulder*. Now he was *here.*

They passed through a sliding door into a warmly lit room with a glowing fireplace. Quasar gestured for him to take a seat in one of the leather sofas, but instead Mace sat stiff at the edge of a chair, unable to relax. Quasar waited patiently as a man dressed in a tux entered with a silver tray holding a pitcher of water and a glass filled with ice cubes. He poured Mace a drink, set everything on a glass-top coffee table, and departed.

"Thank you, Raymond," the masked host said.

Mace and Quasar sat in silence as Mace sipped his water. The quiet felt cozy, welcoming, familiar.

"You have a butler," Mace observed.

The black-helmeted figure tilted its head. "Yes, I have a butler. I also have chefs, a cleaning staff, a battalion of lawyers, houses all over the world, several yachts. Those paintings behind you: they're original Picassos and Van Goghs. But I keep my best artwork at the villas. You should see the Monet over my Monte Carlo bed. And I own a fleet of vehicles that can transform from air to land to sea. Is my wealth really what you're most interested in?"

"So, okay, I'll bite: Why am *I* here? What're you doing all this for?" Mace asked. "Since you already have everything anyone could want?"

"Everything but the perfect pilot," Quasar snapped back. "I want you to race for me."

I want you to . . . Mace's body tingled. He felt warm behind the ears, but he grew still, sinking into his seat. His breathing calmed. "Race? For you?"

"The Gauntlet Prix. I aim to win this year's Glove."

The world's premier sporting event. No, not event. *Extravaganza*. "Wait. The Prix? *This* year?"

"Yes," Quasar said flatly, as if not used to answering questions.

"But why not race yourself? You're a legend!"

"Flattering. I would. But I lost an eye in the crash. I have no depth perception. Winning the Glove in my condition is simply not possible anymore. . . ." Quasar trailed off.

Mace lost himself for a moment trying to imagine what the person behind the opaque visor looked like.

"But I'm only twelve. I don't even have a driver's permit."

"Mozart was doing piano music for kings and queens when he was twelve. What's your point?"

"Um, that I'm not Mozart?" Mace asked.

"He wrote 'Twinkle, Twinkle, Little Star,' you know." Quasar paused. "It's the same tune as the alphabet song."

Mace had to think about that one. He played a few measures of each tune in his head. *A, B, C, D, E, F, G . . .* "Holy cow, you're right!"

Quasar leaned forward. "Your youth is the key, Mace.

The sport's been trending younger for years. It's no secret that younger 'nauts are more fearless, have quicker reflexes. The oldest pilot on the circuit these days is thirty, and he's clearly washed up. My hope is that you *are* Mozart, in your own way."

"Me? Mozart?" His cheeks flushed with sudden pride. "Okay, I like it." He motioned for the praise to continue. "Keep talking."

The famous tune to Mozart's "Requiem" began to rise in volume somewhere from the back of Mace's imagination . . . but scratched to a halt when the mysterious figure spoke up.

"But you're going to have to prove it."

"Huh? I thought I just did."

"There are three other contenders. Over the next several weeks you'll compete against each other for the right to race in the Gauntlet Prix. Only one of you will proceed."

"Hold on." Mace squeezed his temples, grasping for meaning. He felt a stab of fear. He blurted the first excuse that materialized. "How does this . . . ? I have school, and parents, and stuff."

"So do the other three. We'll start when summer break begins."

"And my parents . . . ?" Mace was drowning in sudden doubts.

"What about them?"

"They'll never allow this. They'll think it's dangerous."

Quasar rapped gloved fingertips on the leather armrest. "If I can construct a secret facility under Monument Valley without tipping off the authorities, I think I can handle your mom and dad."

Quasar seemed so certain, but Mace knew TURBO racing was dangerous for an adult—forget about a twelve-year-old. TURBO vehicles crashed in practically every race. And some of those crashes were fatal. Plus, there was something shady about this. He was talking to a masked figure operating out of a secret lair.

"I'm pretty sure I'd have better luck convincing them that Batman wants me to join the Justice League," he said.

"No one says no to me, Mace. My offer will be . . . persuasive. Plus fifty percent of your winnings."

Mace thought hard before answering. The silence stretched out. The fire in the hearth was fed by gas, but he almost imagined he could hear the crackle of real logs. Or maybe he was hearing the sound of his brain overheating. *Winnings*?

He knew: TURBOnauts earned serious coin. No more double shifts for Mom and Dad.

A knock came at one of the doors. "Enter," Quasar called. The door slid into the wall with a hiss, and a finely dressed man with olive skin tone and dark, thick eyebrows nodded to them both. Mace thought he knew this man, but couldn't place him. He turned to the figure in black. "Apologies for the interruption. Your phone calls to select . . . individuals . . . in the Colorado governor's office and the Pentagon . . . have worked. Denver news is reporting the search has been called off. There's no indication whatsoever that Mace is being tracked."

"Thank you, Ahmed." Quasar drew Mace's attention to the man in the doorway. "Meet Ahmed Habadani, Mace. He's my chief mechanic, and he'll be your crew leader."

"'Sup," Mace said, waving, feeling a bit awkward.

"I'm glad you finally made it over to the exhibit." Ahmed winked. "Down to the wire with you."

Mace shot up. The guy who had given him the *Event Horizon* pamphlet on his way out of the mall . . . "You're . . . him! I thought you worked at the arcade."

Ahmed shrugged. "In a manner of speaking, I do. I 'work' at lots of arcades."

"Get him home," Quasar instructed to Ahmed, then turned to Mace. "Ahmed will speak with your parents, arrange everything."

"Wait. Slow down." Mace thought of something.

"No one says 'slow down' to a TURBOnaut," Quasar cautioned.

"Sorry. Just—you need to know something. My parents are deaf," he said.

"So?" Quasar demanded.

Mace was relieved. The news landed like a big nothing burger. Sometimes people could be so weird about it, though. The worst was when they felt sorry for him. He didn't need anyone's pity. That's why he hadn't been in the mood to explain his situation to the girl at the university.

"Makes sense, I suppose," the retired pilot said. "You've been trained your whole life to listen to the world around you in different ways. No wonder you could speak to *Event Horizon* and hear what she had to say."

This is really going to happen. . . . But then he frowned, remembering some advice his dad had shared with him when they were shopping for a used car: *Never rush into a deal, M. If the seller's in a hurry, then they're probably trying to pull one over on you.* And, really, had anyone ever bought a car from someone hiding behind a smoky visor and a black helmet?

"Who are you really, anyway?" he finally asked. "I feel like I'm talking to a Power Ranger."

"First things first," Quasar insisted. "Finish school. You and your parents will sign the paperwork and we'll talk after that."

"I'm supposed to attend a mechanical engineering camp this summer," he revealed. "My parents already put down a deposit—"

"This is the opportunity of your lifetime," Quasar said, cutting Mace off. "You can be a star."

Mace released a deep sigh. What was the point of continuing to play twenty questions? "If you can convince my parents, I'm in."

"You're sure?"

"I'm sure," he stated.

They shook hands.

Mace felt lightheaded with excitement. But he wondered: What had he really just agreed to?

CHAPTER NINE //////

The next week was a blur. The Gerb had left school early. He turned in his report and went off with his dad on their family's amateur TURBO fun-time scavenger hunt of blah. Yawn. Mace was glad he was gone. He never would have been able to keep his mouth shut with Carson constantly yammering about TURBO this and TURBO that.

I WAS THE GUY WHO STOLE EVENT HORIZON *FROM THE AIRPORT! NOW I'M GOING TO BE IN THE GAUNTLET PRIX!* Mace would've eventually blurted, giving away the secret and putting himself in boiling water with Quasar.

Somewhere in the midst of his end-of-the-year parties and tests, the unthinkable happened: Mace's parents *agreed* to let him attend "TURBO Summer Academy."

They had never found out that Mace had left the house that night. He'd snuck back to bed just before dawn, and aside from being a sleepless wreck that day in school, Mace had gotten away with everything. Later, he told his parents, well, a *version* of the truth: that he had won the grand prize in a contest put on by the TURBO simulator company. There would be a scholarship award. Also, he would compete for a chance to pilot a real TURBO craft in a junior circuit relay.

"You sure you want to skip the engineering camp at the U?" Dad had pressed him.

Mace had assured both parents that the TURBO Academy was his best bet for following his dreams. "I'll learn a lot, too. Not just mechanics, but physics, aerodynamics, chemistry."

Mom and Dad had nodded in agreement. "You never get to travel. It'll be good for you to get away from home for part of the summer."

"Is the junior circuit the same as what Robert Gerber competes in?" his mom had asked.

"No." Mace had grinned. "Your boss's league is lower

down. Those guys mostly just race rich-guy vehicles that they're afraid to get dirty."

A sparkle had come to Mom's eyes. Mace had stifled a laugh. She'd really seemed to enjoy that answer.

The morning of departure arrived. Mom made bacon for the occasion and kept pulling Mace close. Dad wore his nicest collared shirt and sat at the table without reading the newspaper.

Ahmed knocked on the door, ready to whisk the "sweepstakes winner" off to sleep-away camp. Mace's parents pulled him into a final group hug on the porch. When they peeled apart, Mom and Dad hurried inside.

"Did you remember your teddy bear?" Ahmed teased as he and Mace turned their backs on the house, hauling suitcases.

"Mr. Wiggle-kisses is packed and ready. So are my picture books. I hope you're good at reading bedtime stories."

Ahmed laughed. "We have people for that."

"Robot skeleton army?" Mace asked.

"Huh?"

"Never mind."

They departed for Denver and caught a private jet to

Monument Valley. Mace was half-mad with anticipation: Who would the other contenders be? If he couldn't outrace all of them, Quasar would send him packing. He wouldn't let that happen.

Ahmed showed him to his underground room. Nothing special, just a bed and a small desk and southwestern cowboy decor. Sleep would have to wait. Ahmed escorted him into the hangar bay, said, "Good luck," and disappeared. The door hissed shut, and Mace heard a latch click.

He frowned. *Good luck with what?* He turned, soaking up what he could see in the hangar.

Four black and gleaming copies of *Event Horizon* were parked front and center. Wow. A fleet of clone trimorphers! Four workbenches had been placed in a line beside the vehicles, each with a tool chest. Mace approached the morphers. His footsteps echoed.

An aircraft morph and a submersible morph were bookended by two roadster morphs. He brushed a hand along the nearest roadster hood, and then he moved to the aircraft. Finally he patted the submersible and the far roadster. He could tell which of the four craft he had piloted here. The feel of each machine was unmistakable and unique.

"Hey there," he spoke to the middle vehicle in aircraft form, stroking her bullet nose affectionately, like the noble steed she was. "I know it's you. Sorry about that hard landing the other night. Ahmed fixed you up perfect, didn't he?"

A door opened, closed. Footsteps. Mace craned around, catching sight of . . . a girl.

"Hello," she said.

He froze.

"You must be . . . one of the others?" she guessed.

"You, too?" said Mace, his throat dry. Her silky black hair was back in a ponytail. She had high cheekbones and an oval face. She wore blue jeans with a fancy woven belt and a button-up shirt with short sleeves. Mace couldn't take his eyes away from her.

"Yes. I'm Aya. Nice to meet you." She held out her hand. "And you are?"

He shook out of his trance. "Hi. I'm . . . Mace."

"Cool," she nodded. "These are nice machines. Perfect copies of the original?"

"Yes, they are," Mace agreed. "But the aircraft morph is the original *Event Horizon*."

"Really? How do you know?"

"Feel right here on all the machines."

Aya moved from the aircraft to the roadsters to the sub, doing what he suggested. She shrugged. "I can't really tell a difference. You sure?"

Mace glanced at his feet. He was sure. But how could he explain it to her?

"Where are you from?" she asked, but before he could even answer, she blurted, "I live in Tokyo and San Francisco. My parents are Japanese, but I'm mostly here in the US."

"I'm from Colorado," Mace admitted, feeling ever-so-ordinary all of a sudden.

"How did you, you know, get caught up in all this?" Mace asked.

"I've been a simulator junkie for years. When *Event Horizon* was on tour in the Bay Area, I couldn't resist a peek. I was so surprised when the canopy closed on me at the museum. Ahmed rescued me from being trapped inside and told me to stay in touch."

"Wait," said Mace. "You didn't have to escape the museum, then fly here?"

Aya laughed. "No. That would've been awesome, though. Can you imagine?"

Yeah, I can. Mace cracked a grin.

"Wait!" she said. "The news last week. The cop chase in Denver. That was you?"

Mace answered her with a guilty smile.

"I saw the footage. That was some great driving." Aya looked a little shaken.

"I had to dodge a missile," he said.

The door hissed open again.

They both whipped around. Two boys entered the hangar on either side of Ahmed. One of them had curly jet-black hair trimmed in a tapered fade. The other was a redhead, freckly and pale. The chief engineer nodded to all of them before leaving.

The newcomers stared at Aya and Mace with suspicion. But Aya either didn't notice or didn't care. She marched over to them, her hand held out. "Hi, I'm—"

"I'm not here to make friends." The redhead cut her off, brushed passed her, and went to stand at one of the four workshop tables. He spoke with an accent that Mace couldn't peg. He was trying to grow a goatee. Red whiskers, more like it. Sparse and scraggly.

"What's this about?" Whiskers asked, popping open a

toolbox and peering inside.

The other boy extended his hand out to Aya's waiting arm. "Hi. I'm Not As Rude As Him."

"Nice to meet you, Not As Rude As Him," Aya replied.

"Ha. Real name's Dex," he added. He also had an accent. "I'm coming from New York, where my uncle has me in school. But I'm originally from the D.R."

"Don't we all come from the doctor?" Mace asked, trying to make a joke. "Originally, I mean?" Everyone stared at him blankly. "Never mind."

"Oh, I get it." Dex laughed. "No, I meant I'm from the Dominican Republic. Next to Haiti. In the Caribbean. You might also know me as Caballero, on the simulator boards."

"Yes! I've raced you!" blurted Mace. "I'm MBlaze07."

"Ah, man! Yeah, I know you. You knocked me off the top spot last week."

"Barely," Mace said. "You're good."

"Wow," said goatee boy, inspecting a torque wrench he'd pulled out of the toolbox on one of the four work tables. "You gonna ask each other for autographs?"

Mace immediately felt like a moron.

"What's your problem?" Dex demanded.

"Listen, kiddos." The redhead addressed all of them. "I've got nothing against any of you. I just happen to think my time is better spent staying ahead of the game than doing icebreakers with kids who are going to be sent packing soon."

"Icebreakers?" muttered Aya. "It's called being polite. You might try it sometime."

The boy shook his head disapprovingly, dropping the torque wrench back in the toolbox. "Wake up. This show's already begun." He pointed upward. Mace followed his gaze. He noted with a stab of anxiety that cameras were set along the ceiling. "If you can't recognize that Quasar's already judging our every move, then you've already lost."

A loud voice rifled through the hangar, startling them all. "Thank you, Henryk, for that introduction."

The disembodied voice of Quasar. Henryk had been right—they were being studied. Mace stiffened. He felt his palms grow clammy. The voice from above continued. "A warm welcome to all four of you. As you know, only one of you will be selected to race professionally."

The four contestants exchanged guarded looks. Mace thought for a moment he might throw up from nerves, but he forced himself to put on a confident face.

Quasar continued. "You will each work alone at one of the four stations. Using only what you have directly in front of you, extract a principal transformer module from any of the trimorpher copies, disassemble it, then reassemble it, and reinstall it. The last of you to correctly reinstall the module will earn a strike. Anyone who earns two strikes goes home."

"Hold on, there," Henryk argued. "I flew all the way out here from Oslo to *race*. What does putting machine parts together have to do with that?"

Ah, Mace noted. *So he's Norwegian.*

Quasar's muffled voice responded. "A professional TURBO-naut knows their vehicle inside and out. You can't react on the course if you don't understand how your machine operates. I realize you may know nothing of engineering, but your performance today will demonstrate to me that you're a fast learner, and that you're nimble enough and logical enough to adapt. You may begin . . . now."

CHAPTER TEN //////

The speaker system cut out, and silence fell over the hangar like a fog. While the others stood by, gathering their thoughts, Mace pounced. He darted over to the aircraft, the original *Event Horizon.* This was *his* trimorpher. They'd been through a lot together. He climbed onto the shoulder of the port-side wing, eyeing an alloy panel he guessed would be hiding the principal transformer module.

Modules were basically fancy gearboxes. They came in two types: principal and auxiliary. Each vehicle housed many auxiliary units, for all the smaller adjustments during morphs. The two principal modules quickly extended and retracted wings. They took a beating during races and were replaced along with tires during pit stops.

Mace sprang open the panel. He'd been right! The unit was a nest of gadgetry, almost a perfect cube. He gave it a pull. It was heavy but glided out of its shell like a sword drawn from a sheath. He slid down the wing and hit the ground running. He dropped the module on his workbench and fished through the toolbox before the others had even worked out where the units were housed.

Dex hopped up on one roadster, Henryk the other. That left Aya with the sub.

Mace took mental photographs of each component as he removed it from the whole. This was precision machinery at its finest. Turning a car into an airplane in less than two seconds required amazing leverage and a surge of incredible power. Some of the parts had names he knew. Gears, clutches, shafts, governors, hubs, cogs, drivers. Power cells. Microchips. Nuts, bolts, washers, grommets. He didn't know what to call a lot of things, though: doohickeys, thingamajigs, whatchamacallits. The cube of interlocking components dissolved into piles of greasy, isolated innards.

He checked on the others now and then, staying a few steps ahead. Henryk was using a socket wrench. Mace hadn't found one in his own tool chest. Each workstation must have different tools. Bad luck for Mace. A socket wrench would've sped things up.

The last components came apart in his hands. "Done taking it apart!" His announcement caused a bit of panic among the others.

Quasar's voice chimed in. "Confirmed. You may proceed with reassembly."

For one horrific moment, Mace scanned the table and had no idea where to begin.

What would Mr. Hernandez tell me? he asked himself. "All right, let's start with the main input shaft." He took a deep breath. He talked himself through each successive piece, building a rhythm and increasing speed.

Aya announced her progress next, and then Dex, and finally Henryk. Frustration was building in Henryk's voice.

Mace hit a snag. The remaining gears he had to insert wouldn't fit anywhere. It took him several minutes to realize he'd previously slid something into place upside down.

He backtracked, taking pieces apart again.

"Done!" Aya called out. She hoisted her assembled module up onto the submersible and inserted it, pumping her fists and breathing a sigh of relief.

Henryk growled with pain, yanking his hand back from a cog that had pinched his finger. The socket wrench jumped from his hand and skidded to a halt on the floor.

Mace stared at it.

Using only what you have directly in front of you . . .

The tool lying *directly* ahead seemed like fair game to Mace.

He darted forward and snatched it up. While Henryk protested, Mace tightened a half dozen final bolts. "Done!" he declared.

"Hey! That's cheating. Give my wrench back. That's mine," argued Henryk.

"What's the matter?" asked Mace. "Thor missing his hammer?"

"Not funny. Give it back."

Mace tossed the wrench to the floor in front of him. "It became mine. It was directly in front of my station. But now it's yours again."

"Doesn't count," Henryk sneered. "You're disqualified."

Mace ignored him, pivoted toward the aircraft, sprang up on the wing, and reinserted the module.

"I've got all the time in the world to finish now," Henryk announced, squaring his shoulders and making a big show of getting back to work.

Mace stayed sitting on the wing. Worry gnawed at him. What if Henryk was right, and Quasar considered his use of the extra tool to be cheating?

The two remaining boys pushed through to the end, neck and neck. Dex squawked excitedly when he completed his module and raced to install it.

Henryk saw that he was last but stood dignified as he tightened his final bolts. He shrugged at one point and cast Mace a dark grin. "All the time in the world," he mouthed. He walked over to the roadster and inserted the gearbox into place.

Quasar entered the hangar, hidden behind the polished helmet with the quasar insignia. The figure pointed for the youths to come together and stood in front of them.

"Aya finished first, followed by Mace, then Dex, then Henryk."

"Mace cheated!" Henryk protested. "He stole my wrench."

"He didn't cheat," Quasar replied. "I heard his explanation. He improvised. He made the rules work for him. And that's my Golden Rule. This is your first lesson, everyone. Hear it well: Rules are strange, bendy things. Make every advantage *your* advantage."

Mace felt uneasy. He was pretty sure the Golden Rule was about treating others the way you'd like to be treated, but he laughed. Nothing had ever come easily to him, yet he always found a way to manage. "I'm your guy."

"We'll see, won't we?" Quasar replied.

Aya and Dex wore frowns. Henryk looked thoughtful.

"You're all twelve," Quasar told them. "Currently, the rules are that TURBOnauts have to be at least sixteen. All of you already exist outside the box. I want my 'naut to *thrive* there."

The hangar grew silent. Quasar waited before continuing. "Aya, board your submersible and morph from water to air to ground on your mount."

Aya lifted the canopy of the sub and climbed aboard. She fired it up, and Mace felt a thrill in his chest as the turbine began to turn and build speed. He saw the same joy awaken in Aya's eyes. Wind and rattling filled the bay. Without warning, and only a whisper of signature noise, the trimorpher transformed atop its pedestal into an aircraft.

"Sweet," Aya exclaimed through the glass. Mace read her lips. He realized: this was probably her first time inside a non-virtual cockpit during a real morph.

"Very good," said Quasar. "Again."

The aircraft morphed without a hitch into a roadster. Mace exhaled. Good for her.

"Henryk, you're next," Quasar told him. The boy nodded confidently, strode over to his roadster, and morphed it twice. Mace felt a stab of disappointment.

"Dex," said Quasar.

He climbed aboard. The aircraft transformed into a sub just fine. But when he toggled to a roadster, a grinding cry belched from inside the hull. Back wheels extended, but the craft dangled off the ground from atop its podium like a speared fish.

Mace's heart lurched.

Henryk let loose a long whistle. "Whew!" he said. "Glad I'm not you."

"Mace, go ahead and take the original *Event Horizon* for a spin," said Quasar.

Everyone waited as he scrambled aboard. *I should have*

double-checked my work! Mace scolded himself. He punched the ignition with his eyes closed. The old-timer fired up like a well-practiced symphony orchestra. He winced each time he morphed, but the sounds that emanated from the vehicle were pitch-perfect. No smoke.

"Mace's transformer module works," Quasar announced. "Dex, your reassembly was flawed. That puts you in last place, behind Henryk. Strike one."

Henryk crowed, "Knew it!"

"I get one more strike, right?" Dex loosened a pretend tie around his neck.

"That was your freebie. Next time you're last, you're out. But I reserve the right to boot anyone at any time for any reason."

Mace felt relieved. Caballero had bested Mace in simulator runs countless times. Getting Dex out of the way early might be best for Mace's chances.

The helmeted figure turned to all of them. "You've each shown me qualities about yourselves. It's time I show you who I am."

"Now we're talking," approved Aya.

"Drumroll, please," added Dex.

Quasar lifted the helmet. Mace drew in a sharp breath.

The injured eye—it was hidden behind a patch. But that's not what made Mace gasp.

Standing opposite him was a gray-haired woman.

////// CHAPTER ELEVEN

Her one green eye shone with such confidence that it distracted from the black eye patch and gnarly burn scars on her neck.

Aya spoke Mace's thoughts. "I thought you were . . . um, a—"

"A man?" Quasar finished for her. "Why does everyone assume Quasar was a man?"

"Man, woman? Who cares?" said Dex. "I'm just glad you don't sound like a stalker anymore, with your helmet off."

"My name is Tempest Hollande," the woman said.

Mace searched his brain. He'd heard the name before. "Hollande Industries," he said. "The TURBO sim company!"

"You're right!" agreed Aya.

"The very least of our products, I assure you. My father was Prescott Hollande. He owned TK Telecommunications."

"Yeah," said Aya. "My parents do business with you. We manufacture medical devices for your health-care companies."

"I know that. I've toured your Osaka factories. I made my fortune with inventions and new technologies. I designed *Event Horizon* all those years ago, and I would *own* this sport today, if it weren't for . . ." She tugged on her collar, revealing more of the scar on her neck. Mace remembered the famous crash that ended her career. "But we'll have our reckoning yet."

"Show us your eye," suggested Henryk.

To Mace's surprise, she did. She turned her patch up to reveal terrible scarring and a cloudy, white pupil shot through with forked, red veins.

"What we're doing comes with risk," said Tempest. She dropped the patch back into place. Mace felt relieved. "You'll be pitted against each other in real machines, traveling at incredible speeds. Things happen out on the track. And I'm asking you to go faster, turn tighter, morph with more precision. You're here to push the envelope of what's possible. If my scars make you queasy, quit now."

"The scars are one thing," Aya muttered. "You lost an eye!"

"And you're lucky I did," Tempest retorted. "Or I'd be out there reclaiming my Glove without your help."

Henryk grinned. "I'll go faster than these—how do you say—yahoos, any day."

"Talk is cheap where I'm from," Dex warned.

"Whatever. Just go back to Jamaica now," Henryk suggested. "Save yourself the embarrassment of having to eat your words."

"What?" laughed Dex. "Dude. I'm *Dominican*. Should I tell you to go back to Sweden?"

Tempest came between them. "That's enough, boys. Sort it out on the track. For now, you're dismissed to your quarters. Read the manuals you find on your desks. Memorize them front and back. There will be tests. I expect all of you to get one hundred percent on all of them. Or else."

CHAPTER TWELVE /////

The four prospective TURBOnauts gathered for the day's first meal.

Four days into training and cramming for tests—memorizing everything from Gauntlet Prix stats to jet-propulsion science—all the rivals complained of exhaustion. But Aya looked the part this evening. Her hair was pulled back in a messy ponytail. Her eyes were puffy. "I'm not sleeping well," she admitted. She looked like she might cry. "At all, really."

"It's okay," said Henryk, chomping off the end of a

breakfast burrito. "In a couple of days, you can catch up on all the sleep you want."

"Training all night, sleeping all day," Aya snapped back. "I'm not an owl."

They were becoming nocturnal, training at night so they wouldn't be seen. The fluorescent lights were their cue that it was time to rise and shine. Mace couldn't ignore the faint electric crackle that came with the overhead lighting. It sounded to him like a dental drill was forever in the next room, probing someone's teeth.

Mace had made himself three burritos. He scarfed one down and continued with his mouth full. "You're probably catching more z's than you realize."

"I don't know." Aya saw that her hair was in her food. Or maybe it was her food in her hair. Mace couldn't decide which; she picked at one or the other. "Even down here, my body knows the difference between night and day. Isn't that happening to you?"

Mace gulped down some OJ. "Of course! Remember how cranky I was yesterday? You lasted a day longer than I did!" Truth was, it took him a while to fall asleep each day, but he was finally getting used to it.

Aya sighed explosively.

"Try moving to northern Norway during the summer," Henryk suggested unhelpfully. "Sun never sets."

"Have you seen the northern lights?" Mace asked him.

Henryk nodded. "In the winter, when the sun never rises."

"That's cool," said Mace, trying to imagine such an exotic place as Norway. That country had TURBO courses; he'd get to go there someday.

"Did you try sleeping different ways?" Dex asked Aya. "I have to find the right position, till it works. Sometimes I . . ." He climbed up onto an empty cafeteria table and demonstrated his method, bending his elbows backward and dangling a leg to the floor. He tucked a wrist behind his back. "Like this."

"You look like a grilled chicken." Henryk laughed.

"After living through four hypercanes, I can sleep anywhere," Dex said.

"What?" everyone asked at once.

Hypercanes were a step above a hurricane. They could develop without warning, building winds as high as three hundred miles an hour. The Caribbean was getting blasted by them yearly these days. Something to do with the ozone layer falling apart—or something—but that's all Mace knew about it.

"I've been through four," Dex said. "During one, my sister and I were the only kids in my neighborhood to make it."

"To make it?" gulped Mace. "As in, to *survive*?"

Dex gave a grim nod. "We got lucky."

Mace dropped his second burrito. "And I thought snow storms in May were annoying."

"So sorry, man," Aya offered.

"After the last hyper, power was out across the island for four months. The laws got relaxed for travel. Uncle Ricky brought me and my sis to New York, put us in the school he teaches at."

"So, when I send you packing"—Henryk turned back to Dex, his mouth full of breakfast burrito—"are you going to use your loser money to live in New York or to go back to Natural Disaster Land?"

Dex spit out the orange juice he was drinking.

Aya glared at the Norwegian. "I could teach a university course on how obnoxious you are."

"Shame I won't have time to take your class," Henryk sneered. "I'll be too busy winning."

Dex leaned forward. "The only contest you've won so far is the dumb goatee contest."

"I'm not here to be friends," Henryk said. "Only one of us can win."

"You're wrong," Mace argued. "People can compete and still get along."

Dex agreed. "What's the point of winning if you have no friends?"

"Um . . . MONEY," Henryk answered. "And fame. And glory. And the thrill of being worshipped. But you guys go be besties. I'll go win the Glove. It's fine with me."

Tempest's voice came over the loudspeaker. "Five minutes. Meet me in the bay. A lot to cover today before we finally get you behind the wheel."

"Five minutes?" griped Mace. "But I'm still so hungry."

"Eat up," said Henryk. "It's the only thing you're really fast at."

Mace's and Henryk's eyes locked on each other. Without looking away, Mace picked up his burrito and took a huge bite. He chewed while staring down the Norwegian. Henryk lifted his own burrito and tore at it angrily with his teeth. He chewed, swallowed, and gulped down some OJ. His next bite was even more fierce. He grinned. Bits of egg, sausage, and potato stuck to his chin.

Mace swallowed his mouthful, and then shoved the rest of his burrito in his mouth in one bite.

Dex and Aya stopped eating and watched the two boys competing to see who could inhale their food fastest.

Mace smacked Dex's shoulder. "More burritos." Food erupted from his mouth as he gave orders. "And juice."

"You're on," Henryk spat. He gave Aya a glance and gestured toward the burrito bar.

Aya and Dex shared a brief look, then both of them bolted for the leftover food. Mace and Henryk scarfed what remained on their plates. Dex and Aya slammed new trays down in front of them, each with five more burritos.

Feverishly chewing and swallowing, the rivals ate and ate. Faster and faster. Mace refused to let Henryk gain ground. He paced Henryk until something in his stomach churned sickly. He downed more OJ. Never stopping. Faster. More speed. They were both down to their last burrito, their shirts caked with egg and salsa and orange pulp.

Tempest burst into the dining room, confused at first, then disgusted. The kids fell silent, though Mace and Henryk continued to chow down their final burritos.

"What are you doing?" Tempest demanded.

Mace couldn't have answered if he'd wanted to. He'd crammed the last bite of food into his mouth. He slammed back a cup of OJ. Swallowed.

His plate was empty. His mouth was empty. Henryk was still chewing.

"Checkered flag is all mine!" he shouted triumphantly, raising clenched fists into the air.

Henryk reached over and smacked Mace in the stomach with an open palm.

Orange juice and salsa rose into the back of Mace's throat and shot up his nose. The sting of it was too much.

He puked all over the table.

Everyone jumped back. Henryk swallowed his last bit, caught a breath, almost choked, held it back, and started laughing.

"You didn't hold it down," Henryk declared. "That means I win!"

Mace was coughing. His eyes watered and his throat stung. He looked at the table, and what he saw almost brought up another round of half-chewed breakfast.

Tempest grabbed Henryk by the sleeve and pulled him away. She ushered everyone but Mace out of the dining room. “He’s right,” she told him as they all funneled out, leaving Mace bent over, alone, with his hands propped on his knees. “You lost. Clean it all up.”

“Come on!” he managed, finally catching his breath. “He hit me!”

“No. He took advantage. How many times do I have to point this out?” Tempest said. “Hitting your opponents hard is how you’re going to win.”

CHAPTER THIRTEEN //////

The rivals were finally facing off. They were already fifteen laps into the twenty-six-lap-long course that Tempest had staged above the Utah desert. Dawn was approaching, and the pink sky was filled with fiery red clouds. This aircraft battle counted. The loser would earn a strike. Dex was at risk of going home.

"What happens if you lose speed on a sharp turn and the compressor blades don't self-recover?" Ahmed asked in Mace's helmet headset.

Pop-quiz time, Mace thought. The point of these

questions was twofold: Could Mace recall important basics of flight training while under high stress? And, could he walk and chew gum at the same time? Carrying on a conversation while rocketing through the atmosphere was a skill that took some practice.

"I'd feel the airflow adjustment stagnate," he answered through his mic. "Don't wait. Just shut 'er down and reboot."

"That's the textbook answer," Ahmed replied.

In the first twenty laps, Mace had never once dropped into last place. He'd been in first or second for most of the race. Aya and Dex were easy to handle, their attempts at passing him predictable and too by the book.

Dex inched up behind him again, and—yup—tried to sneak by on the inside of the next hovering checkpoint. Mace cut him off.

A new voice rang in his ears. "Blast jet exhaust in his face!" Tempest ordered. "Pump oil into the chamber, like I taught you. It'll burn thick and black, blotting out the sky."

"What?"

"Do it. Smoke screens aren't allowed, but there's no punishment for a temporary malfunction."

"But this is on purpose!"

"No one can prove it, if you do it just like I instructed."

Mace frowned, but he followed orders. His craft belched black fumes, and Dex lost speed and altitude.

"Excellent, Mace!" cried Tempest.

"I've never seen anyone do that in a race," he grumbled.

"Exactly," explained Tempest. "That's why you'll get away with it. Now get up on Henryk."

Mace had to admit Henryk was fast. Solid, confident, unshakable. No matter how well Mace executed each bend in the air track, Henryk matched him lap for lap. He and Mace duked it out for the lead in a constant weave. Mace couldn't break free of him.

"Be forewarned: I've taught him a trick or two as well," Tempest added.

What? Mace felt confused. TURBO racing was about speed, not booby traps.

Twenty-five laps. Morning had arrived. The sun peeked above the horizon, and Mace had to squint through the burst of light on the next turn. Tempest's voice fed into his helmet. "Last lap. You all should be fighting tooth and nail for that win!"

Mace felt his engine sputter, grasping at the thin air. He

nudged a few dials, and felt his thrusters catch. *Perfect,* he thought. But the pat on his own back was too soon. Henryk pulled ahead, vanishing into the blue!

"No," Mace growled. "Get back here." He pushed the engine for everything it had, setting Henryk square in his mental crosshairs. It wasn't working. Henryk took every bank just a little tighter than he could, inching farther and farther away.

What am I doing wrong? he thought. His indicators were all within normal.

Don't sweat it. Let him go. Take an easy second place and call it a day.

Mace thought for a moment. *Second place? Let Henryk win?* "No way. Not happening."

He gave the afterburner more fuel.

The steering wheel shook. Mace's neck strained. He scarcely touched the wheel, allowing the wing flaps to do the work for him. Beyond Henryk, up ahead, through the glare of the rising sun, Mace could make out the checkered finish line, held up by hovering drones.

I can do it, he thought. *I can inch by him just in time. . . .*

He hit the throttle hard, blasted forward like a rocket.

Coming up on Henryk, Mace squeezed the steering wheel harder than he needed to. "Come on. Steady," he scolded himself. "You've got—whoa!" An external casing had dislodged from Henryk's hull! It flew at Mace like a bullet. He had to jerk upward suddenly in time to clear the debris. His left rear drift fin sprang wide for stabilizing support. Mace leaned into the heavy ascent, his mind on fire.

He did that on purpose! Could have killed me!

"Mind your compressor," came Ahmed's warning.

Too late. The gauges flashed, an alarm sounded, and Mace stalled.

"What!?" he yelped. The engine control flooded. Henryk's dirty trick might kill him yet! His seat jerked, and the canopy view turned upside down. The sky was replaced by ground.

Mace studied his readouts. "I stalled out!"

Tempest wasn't interested in protests. "Watch your cabin pressure. Make engine adjustments accordingly."

Mace had done his reading. He'd aced the tests. He knew how to handle this. The protocol came automatically. "Shut down. Reboot." He held tight, trusting his training. The engine turned over, sputtered, grabbed oxygen, and died.

Mace was suddenly in complete free fall, the pink Utah desert growing larger and larger all around him. "What?!" he yelled. *I did everything right!* "What do I do?!"

Tempest came on the radio. "A bit of Henryk's debris get in your manifold?"

How could she sound so calm right now? "Help me!"

"Make repairs."

"Mid-flight?" said Mace. "Like I'm supposed to climb out on the hood and give 'er an oil change?"

But he snapped out of his panic. *Okay,* he thought. *Shut down again. Reboot again. This time, do a diagnostic before pressing the ignition . . . .*

Alarms buzzed. Red lights flashed.

He shut the engine down. Ran the engine tests.

PROCESSING

PLEASE WAIT

Aya and Dex overtook his position while he tumbled, while the computer twiddled its thumbs.

So much for placing first. So much for placing at all.

The question now was simply one of survival.

OBSTRUCTION IN MAIN VENT. DECOMPRESS?

YES NO

“Yes! Yes!” Mace shouted. He pushed the matching word on the screen. There was a hissing and a pop. Good. Now he could turn this thing back on, maybe salvage a third-place finish.

How *dare* Henryk pull a dirty move like that? Mace vowed to get him back.

If he lived, that was.

IMPACT IMMINENT

The ground . . . It was coming at him . . . like a planet-sized train!

EJECT! EJECT!

He yanked on the ejection lever. Locked! Where was the release? The desert floor! Mace gripped his helmet, wished it all away. He cursed Henryk’s name. The last thing he saw: blood spraying the spiderwebbed windshield in thick sheets—and then it was over.

////// CHAPTER FOURTEEN

Blood. Everywhere. *Oh, nice touch,* Mace thought. He slammed his palms on the steering wheel. The state-of-the-art screens faded to black. The gruesome scene vanished.

GAME OVER

STATUS: DNF—CASUALTY

Did. Not. Finish. Also known as last place. Aka strike one for Mace Blazer.

He turned off his radio headset and cursed into his helmet.

He could've placed second, no problem. Why had he risked so much just to shame Henryk?

He knew the answer: Because he didn't want to be second. He wanted to be first.

A long pause followed. He removed the helmet, ran a hand through his sweaty hair. The door opened automatically. Light poured into the simulator cockpit. Tempest and Ahmed stood against the opening, silhouettes beneath headsets.

"These graphics are too realistic," Mace said. "The summary screen should read: 'Status: Condor Breakfast Buffet.'"

"Condors need a carcass to feed on. You're more like a beef stew," Ahmed said. His tone became critical. "You're awfully glib for a dead man."

A commotion erupted in the room beyond. The other three competitors tumbled out of their simulators. The room was dominated by four game pods, each suspended with independent spider legs anchored to the concrete floor. Aya and Dex emerged, cautiously pleased with themselves. They wove through interlaced simulator supports to reach Mace. Dex looked relieved. Henryk popped out of his machine and tossed both hands high in the air. "Kick the tires and light the fires!" Henryk bragged. "Thank you, ladies and gentlemen. And you're welcome. *That* is how it's done."

"You're impossible." Aya turned her back on the Norwegian.

"It's all part of his strategy to throw you off," Mace pointed out. "You can't let it get to you."

"What happened to you?" Dex asked.

Mace narrowed his eyes. "He got to me. Flung debris in my face. I dodged, lost engine control, died."

"Oh, and you didn't spit black smoke in my eyes?" Dex challenged.

Mace hated that Dex was right. How was he supposed to complain about Henryk, when making everyone else crash seemed to be what Tempest was teaching them to do? "I'm sorry, Dex."

"Don't be sorry," Tempest said. "Winners don't apologize. Henryk's not sorry."

"I'm not sorry," agreed Henryk, grinning.

"When are we going to face off in the real trimorphers?" Mace asked Tempest, his shoulders squared, stepping up to her. "Your simulators are good, but they're not the same as the real thing."

Tempest turned her head and gripped a hand around

the nearest spidery simulator leg. "Are you trash-talking my personally designed, very expensive TURBO simulators, Mr. Blazer?"

Mace shrank back, but only a little bit. "I can feel the difference. This daddy long-legs doesn't feel the same as *Event Horizon* does. Trying to accelerate when I'm really stationary isn't working for me anymore."

"'Feel the same?'" mocked Henryk. "It's all excuses. Cheap talk."

"Shut up, Henryk. Mace is right." Tempest awarded him an approving nod.

Mace laughed.

"What's so funny?" Tempest demanded.

"I just checked the internet," Mace cracked. "Hashtag ShutUpHenryk is trending!"

The Norwegian lunged at him, but Ahmed got between them.

"Listen to me," Ahmed said. "I know you want to jump in real cockpits. But we have to prepare you for various bad weather conditions. Only the sims can prepare you for that. It's not out of the question that we'll run into thick fog in San

Francisco, or cyclone conditions in the Philippines. Races are expensive; they almost never get canceled. It's important to always know how to react."

Tempest pursed her lips, then shook her head. "Those adjustments should be intuitive for these geniuses. I'd rather we spend what time we have left reinforcing the value of the Golden Rule."

Ahmed raised an eyebrow in disagreement. "Tempest, may I speak with you in private for a—"

"No. We're done with the simulators starting now," she decided. "A few more days of individual instruction and you'll race each other for keeps during a real desert competition. Dex and Mace, you better watch your backs. One more strike, and you're gone."

Mace wasn't too worried. He couldn't wait to show the others how fast he could go behind the wheel of the genuine *Event Horizon*. "Roger that." He gave her a stiff salute.

Dex put on a brave face. "Believe me, I've gotten out of tighter spots in my life."

Tempest continued. "I'll enter whoever remains in the Philippines Cross-Country Showcase. It's Amateur League, but their vehicles are generally high performing. I expect you all to take the top slots. The only question is, which of you will place first? The winner goes on to the Gauntlet Prix."

"We're going to the Philippines?" Mace asked. World travel. Another perk of this glamorous lifestyle. He couldn't wait.

And then it occurred to him: Carson Gerber's dad competed in that league. What if they ended up racing each other?

Aya appeared upset. "We're not going to practice with dicers?" she asked.

Some trimorphers were more specialized than *Event Horizon*, turning into helicopters rather than fixed-wing aircraft. Dicers. Other models became speedboats instead of submersibles. Those were called skimmers. Dicers were slower than fixed-wing morphers, so their courses branched off, and those pilots had to compete on tighter tracks before joining everyone else on the roads.

"Helicopter morphers are only just beginning to appear in the pro league, Aya. We've been over this. Dicers are hardly taken seriously when it comes to nabbing the Glove."

Aya pursed her lips. "I've always been best with dicers. I wish you'd give me the chance to prove it to you."

Tempest watched Aya closely but said no more on the subject.

The others trickled out of the simulator bay. Tempest pulled Mace aside.

"You don't owe anybody anything. Henryk's right about you and Dex and Aya becoming too close. You can't hesitate when the time comes. You can't be sorry."

"This is all I ever wanted, to be a part of this," Mace said, raising an eyebrow. "I'm giving it everything I have."

"You have to want to be *on top* of it, not a *part* of it. If your goal is just to be *in* a TURBO race, then the Glove is already lost. I want you to come at this whole sport sideways. The cops, over Denver, they called you a renegade. Remember? That's what I'm looking for. Something sensational. Something revolutionary. You're here to wreck the careers of those you've always admired. I want you to bury the competition."

But Mace was only half listening. He was already imagining himself winning the Glove. "Renegade. I like that. Mind if I take it as my racing name?"

"You have to earn it first," she answered. "And don't forget—you already have one strike against you."

CHAPTER FIFTEEN //////

The fire flickered on the hearth beside the coffee table, warming the right side of Mace's all-black jumpsuit. He'd slipped into it for the first time only moments ago. The boots had extra thick soles for some reason. "Why'd you make me so tall?" he asked Tempest. "Feels weird." His voice reverberated throughout his closed visor.

"So you can reach the pedals, and so you don't look so twelve in front of the cameras." They stood eye to eye. "Just trust in my infinite wisdom."

The others entered one by one, hidden behind glossy

black helmets. Mace honestly couldn't tell who was who. They were carbon copies of one another, same as Tempest's fleet of copycat *Event Horizons*.

The kids took seats near the fire, placing their personal tablets on the table. Mace could tell Henryk by his body language. He was acting like he owned the room, taking over an entire sofa for himself. Aya was the first to reveal herself. Her long black hair fell down around her shoulders as she lifted her mask. Mace couldn't look away from her. "This is too creepy," she said.

Dex also removed his helmet. "I don't know. I think it's kind of cool. I feel like we're bank robbers. And this is the calm before the big heist."

"I wouldn't rob a bank with you slowpokes," said Henryk, ditching his helmet and running a hand through his wavy red hair. He rested a leg on his opposite knee and sank into his couch. "Have any of you heard how this is going to work tonight?"

The nighttime, real-desert competition was almost upon them. "If I had advance information about the race, you think I'd share it with you?" said Mace.

"Good point. I almost forgot: you don't like to play fair."

"I'm just following orders, same as you." Mace held on to

his anger. *Get him back on the terrain,* he thought.

"I haven't heard a word," Dex offered.

"Me neither," Aya said. "Aside from the route we were given to study."

"Did we all get the same map?" Mace wondered.

"Good question," said Dex. All four of them lifted their tablets and opened their route maps and compared them. Mace reviewed the route one more time as he pored over the interactive map. One giant loop alternating between the ground and air over the desert, with a segment of underwater track through the black canyon depths of Lake Powell. The directions would be uploaded to his live display, but he wanted to have every bend and turn of the sprawling desert course memorized.

"Hey, my map is blank," Aya pointed out. "That's weird."

"It is? Here, check mine," said Mace.

"Thanks."

"Hey, guys," said Dex carefully. "Is anyone else bothered by all the little cheats Tempest is teaching us? It's distracting. I just want to go out there and floor it."

"No," answered Henryk immediately. "She's just giving us the tools to win."

"Yeah. It's not TURBO racing, though," Dex said. "It's a demolition derby. Her Golden Rule stinks."

Mace watched Dex closely. How could he be saying that? What if Tempest was listening?

"Someone could get hurt the way she tells us to bash each other around," Aya agreed. "I mean, Mace already *died* once."

"I got better," Mace reminded them.

Dex put out his hand, motioned for everyone else to join him. "Let's make a pact. No funny stuff out there tonight. We win the right way."

Aya thrust her arm forward, slapped her gloved hand on top of Dex's. Mace bit his lip. He wanted to join them. But only if Henryk was on board. He looked to Henryk and noted a mischievous glint in his eyes. "I'll agree to that," Henryk eagerly said. He jumped up. "I don't need to cheat to win!" Mace was the only holdout. "See?" mocked Henryk. "He knows he can't win an honest race."

"That's not it." This sucked. What was Mace supposed to do? Aya gave him an impatient look.

He didn't want to disappoint her. "I'm in," he grumbled. He put his hand forward and completed the chain. He managed to sneak his palm under Dex's, where it could give Aya's hand a squeeze.

Ahmed appeared beside the hearth through one of the sliding doors. "It's time," he announced.

They disbanded quickly. Mace wouldn't meet anyone's gaze. He felt guilty, as if he'd been caught with his hand in a cookie jar.

He adjusted his one-piece flight suit and hooked his black helmet under an arm. The butterflies in his stomach turned to a swarm of fire ants.

"Tempest and I will be on comm with all four of you all the time," Ahmed explained. "But there's no crosstalk between rivals allowed in a real race, and you won't be permitted to communicate directly with each other tonight, either."

They nodded their understanding.

Tempest met them in the hangar. She wore a smug grin, and Mace immediately saw why.

Event Horizon and two copycats were parked in roadster form side by side in the cavernous bay. A fourth trimorpher was with them. It had no paint job. Helicopter blades were folded back and tucked into the naked roadster's body.

"What's that?" Aya asked, cautiously hopeful.

"It's your ride," Tempest confirmed.

Aya squealed her delight.

Tempest gave her a hard look. "Review your tablet now. Your dicer route has been uploaded. It'll be on your dash, too. You better perform well tonight."

Aya's excitement vanished, replaced by a flash of alarm. She realized everyone was watching her reaction, and she tightened her expression. "I'll do better than ever, like I said I would. I'll prove it." She lost herself studying her new course.

"So, how is this going to work?" asked Henryk.

"Everyone stick to your practice models," Tempest explained.

Aya looked up. "I'm starting from scratch," she said.

"True," Tempest said. "But you wanted this. And I'll award you a head start. Henryk and Aya: You have zero strikes, so you may begin," Tempest answered.

Henryk and Aya gave each other a long look. Then it clicked: the green flag had dropped! They ran for their vehicles and leaped inside their cockpits. They pressed dashboard buttons, and their canopies lowered. The engines came alive, filling the concrete bay with a deafening roar, rattling Mace's rib cage.

Aya was first away, peeling out of the hangar and up through the long rampway to the outside world. Henryk was right behind her, leaving a double line of burnt tire treads behind.

Mace shared a sour look with Dex. So, this race was really two matchups, then? Aya versus Henryk. And later, Mace would duel Dex. Did that mean either Mace or Dex was definitely going home tonight?

I want you to bury the competition.

This was all by design, Mace knew. But Dex was his friend. This would be hard.

"All right, boys," Tempest said. "You may begin."

Mace's heart jackhammered. "What? Already?"

"It's one race," she clarified, "and you two have some catching up to do."

Mace stood gawking, with shock and gathering despair. *One matchup!* he thought. *And we're starting this far behind?*

"I'd get going if I were you," Tempest suggested in the silence that followed.

The silence of a lost cause.

Mace and Dex slammed on their helmets and bolted toward their waiting roadsters.

////// CHAPTER SIXTEEN

Mace beat Dex to the punch. He spiraled *Event Horizon* up the long, narrow tunnel toward the outer world. The going was slow. Mace was poor at drifting—speeding forward while turning in the direction of the curved tunnel. Henryk and Aya's lead might be growing. He gritted his teeth and shot ahead as fast as he dared.

Then the starry night came into view. He punched through the exit, out the monument's rock face, and accelerated along the dark landing strip of the open desert floor, desperate to close the gap with the leaders.

Where were they?

There. Henryk's afterburners lit up the night sky as he rose into the distant air. Aya had taken off as a helicopter. Her air routes were shorter, with more drone-assisted hoops to navigate. She'd meet back up with the boys at the next morph site.

They were so far ahead already!

Think, Mace, he cautioned himself. The end of the runway approached, and he slapped the ground-to-air morph a split second before his display advised him to do so. He lifted off the road and went airborne, smooth and steady, as he had been practicing all week. He banked sharply left to stay on course.

Dex was coming up beside him. *No, you don't,* Mace scolded, and veered to box him out.

Mace found Henryk. Black against the stars, he could feel the invisible cone of calm air produced by Henryk's jet—his wake—and placed himself within it. Mace's flying grew steadier. Riding a leader's wake was how geese saved energy for migrations.

Duck, duck, goose. Mace accelerated, closing the distance.

The high desert was a blur below him, moonlit, the horizon full of shadowy silhouettes of tall rock formations. They approached a stone arch—a mandatory checkpoint. Henryk slowed, navigating the hole cautiously. Was Henryk chickening out? Mace laughed. *Event Horizon* gained. The diameter was tight. It'd be close. This was no ordinary checkpoint hoop. It wouldn't budge if he clipped it. "Nudge a little more to the left. No slowing," Mace told himself. He corrected his steering ever so slightly, and blasted out the other side of the rock arch.

Dex slowed behind him, but Caballero in his rearview hardly mattered. Mace's single focus was catching up to Henryk.

Ahmed startled him in his helmet's earpiece. "Diagnostics look steady, Mace. Remember your training, and make every morph matter."

Mace heard Aya's voice through Ahmed's receiver. Ahmed cut the transmission, but not before Mace caught her asking for navigational confirmation for her upcoming air-to-ground touchdown.

Henryk was already back on the road. Mace would have to hit the same landing mark or be docked a time penalty. "Going in," he informed Ahmed.

"Watch for Aya. She's incoming, too."

"Got it," he said. And there she was like a hawk coming down, fast and precise, on a field mouse.

Mace emptied his mind and morphed to ground.

The wings tucked in; the wheels dropped. Turbulence followed, and then *Event Horizon* touched down a split second behind Aya. Sparks flew. She swerved as her rotator blades folded in. Mace cheered for her, forgetting that he had dropped into third place.

"That was near perfect! Ahmed, give her props for me."

"High-five her later. No crosstalk."

A proximity alert beeped. He checked his rear display. Dex was still on his tail, closing, eager to pass. Mace ignored him, thinking only forward. *Get in front of Aya. And then Henryk.*

Aya's taillights were like demon eyes in the dark ahead. Mace squinted. He could sense the vehicle; the rumble of its wheels on the cracked pavement somehow vibrated up through his core. "Let's practice passing, shall we?" He shifted, accelerated, and came up on her rapidly. Mace swerved onto the narrow highway's left lane and zoomed up beside her.

The two drivers studied each other across the night,

hidden behind their visors, but illuminated by their dashboard displays. He gave the roadster's pedal a shove and gained on her, but she matched his speed.

The turn took Aya by surprise. She hadn't memorized the map like Mace had, and when he cut the corner tight, he was able to pull ahead of her.

The battle for third was now between Aya and Dex. Mace focused on the win.

Henryk's taillights grew nearer. Mace felt like he was *wearing* his vehicle now. He commanded it forward—faster, faster—with every synapse in his body. And the trimorpher responded to his movements the way a shoe obeys the foot. He and the craft were one, their breathing and their pulse the same. He zoomed over the empty, winding highway at the edge of Lake Powell, and when Henryk veered left to block him—as Mace knew he would—Mace cut right and passed him.

Just like that, Mace was in the lead! He let out a shout. But the finish line wasn't in sight yet. His vision was crisp, his thinking fluid. His muscles thrummed with energy.

"Keep focused," he warned himself.

The first water entry was coming up. Lake Powell was a bottomless, black abyss, with cliff faces and stone formations rising from its surface. Once a labyrinth of canyons, now the Colorado River filled in the sandstone gulfs. It was *deep*. A deadly maze.

Henryk would be cautious navigating the chasms. If Mace could find the courage to go all in, he could press his advantage.

But he was unsure in the water. All week, his practice entries had been shaky. He remembered the reservoir at the Boulder airport, how *cold* the water had been, flooding the cockpit . . .

He passed a road sign for the boat ramp. Mace checked his control panels, which were dimmed to keep the glare off the curved window surfaces. All sensors were green. He was clear for water entry. He felt his heart rate quicken.

Ahmed's voice crackled in his headphones. "Maintain speed into the sharp turn, then I want to see a flawless morph."

But Mace botched the hairpin turn, catching a patch of loose sand on the pavement. He fishtailed off the road, kicking up grit.

Henryk eased past him.

"Crud!"

"It's not over yet," Ahmed cautioned.

The glassy, midnight-blue surface of the lake loomed

large. It took every ounce of willpower not to tap the brakes.

"Power up!" Ahmed shouted.

Mace obeyed, giving the vehicle extra fuel. He felt *Event Horizon* accelerate. He was on the ramp, at water's edge. He morphed . . .

. . . and the tires folded up into the hull too early. The underbelly scraped against the concrete ramp, but momentum carried it forward until the vehicle hit the water.

The deceleration was intense. Mace's smart cushioning grabbed him tight, keeping his body from flying forward through the canopy.

Aya, and then Dex, passed him by.

The turbine extended and kicked in. Mace was beneath the lake. He was moving at high speed through near blackness. His headlights only gave shape to what was right in front of him.

"Ahmed, it's pitch-black down here."

"Trust yourself. You can do this."

Mace closed his eyes and *listened*. In the way a radio antenna listens. He imagined that he could feel the submerged canyon walls below him, the rock pinnacles and spires rising from the depths like stalagmites. The vibrations of the vehicle moved through the water and bounced off these objects and surfaces and reached back to him. He could tell their shape, how far away they were.

Mace ignored the displays entirely. He kept his eyes closed, leaned on the throttle.

He came up behind Henryk. The Norwegian was going awfully slow. *Choke!* Passing him was almost disappointing. But there was no time to gloat. There were still two more leaders to overtake.

Dex was next. Mace used the smooth cone of the forward trimorpher's wake to approach at full force. He waited right behind Dex for a moment, then jogged abruptly left. Dex took the bait. He veered left to block Mace's path, but Mace had already swerved up and back to the right. He inched farther and farther ahead. Dex wanted to box him out and knocked him with his hull. Mace pushed back. He could feel where the turbulence diminished and glided into the smoother water currents. It was Dex who was boxed out, forced to cut through the patchy knots where warmer and colder lake water mixed. It was like a race car owning the road while an opponent drove with two wheels on the shoulder.

Mace pulled ahead. He increased his lead, and left Dex struggling in the dark.

The end of the race was growing near, but Aya was still far in the lead.

He pressed forward, searching for her vehicle's signature in the water.

Just as he detected her up ahead, she disappeared.

"Dang it!" Mace spat. This was not good. Aya had broken out of the water, going airborne again.

All that remained of the race was a final sprint back to the facility runway. Aya's approach would be shorter than his.

First one to enter the hangar would win. Given the distance remaining, Mace's chances of overtaking Aya in the air were extremely slim.

"This is it, Mace." Tempest was on his comm. "This is her first run in a dicer. You should be embarrassed. Let her beat you, and I'll send you home."

"You gave her a huge head start!" Mace argued.

"So, what're you going to do about it? Show me some steel, Mace Blazer. Show me you want to win—no matter what."

Mace flipped off his comm. He cursed in anger. He had made a deal with his friends! But Mace had no choice. He had to break his word.

CHAPTER SEVENTEEN /////

Water-to-air morphs were the easiest and safest transitions of all. Mace trusted his vehicle. He increased speed and launched back into the sky. Within seconds, his canopy was dry, his view clear of water streaks, and he found himself flying low over the pale, moonlit sandstone formations. He turned southeast and punched the afterburner over Monument Valley.

Aya was off on her own course again. Mace couldn't spare any attention to the details. He had to look forward. Think forward. Lean forward.

He hit every hoop at top speed, taking the turns tight. But Aya matched him move for move, pushing through her shorter zigs and zags without losing time.

And now there it was: the secret facility landing strip, soft blue lighting leading into the rock formation. The first of them to touch down and reenter the cliff face and reach the interior hangar would be declared the victor. Aya was in the lead—and going in for the final landing.

Think! he demanded of himself. He opened a channel to Ahmed. "What do I do?"

Aya's voice caught his ear. "Eleven percent declination. No crosswind."

"You're on target," he heard Ahmed confirm before he pivoted to Mace. "Not looking good for you."

Mace recalled that Ahmed and Tempest were running point for all four of them! Mace couldn't open a direct line to Aya. But maybe he could get to Aya through Ahmed.

I want my 'naut to thrive *outside the box.*

Rules are strange, bendy things. Make every advantage your *advantage . . .*

"I know!" he shouted into his headset.

"Know what?"

"It's jammed, Ahmed! What do I do?"

"What's jammed?"

"My port aileron is jammed. I can't compensate! There's a fire. I'm gonna crash!"

"Uh, my sensors don't indicate—"

"AHMED, I CAN'T STEER!"

"Stand by." The chief engineer's voice was focused. Mace listened as Ahmed spoke to Aya. "Abort landing. I repeat. Abort landing. *Event Horizon* in distress. Need a visual on his portside wing. Possible fire. Possible flap obstruction."

"Are you serious?" Mace heard Aya bark. "Fine. Aborting. Rerouting. Tell him to stay calm and fly straight as he can. I'll pull up beside his port." The transmission cut out.

Mace suddenly felt nauseated. What was he doing? Aya would be livid about this.

He grunted in agony. But what choice did he have?

Ahmed spoke in Mace's ear. "Hang in there. She's—"

"Oh, hey, look," he cut Ahmed off. "Everything's working fine all of a sudden. Imagine that." Mace severed his own radio.

Aya had abandoned her approach to the landing strip. She'd slowed and risen, ready to fall back beside Mace in aid.

An opening a TURBOnaut could only dream of.

"You wanted to see some steel? How's this for a steal?"

Mace punched it. As he shot by Aya from below, his canopy clipped her emerging rear left tire, sending it flying into the dark. The windshield cracked. His displays flickered. The landing angle was too steep! Morphing gadgetry deep within the craft clicked and reset. Mace's wheels smacked the landing checkpoint hard. He fishtailed on the dusty runway, then gained subtle control. The rock wall opened—and thank the gods of speed and adrenaline that it did—because Mace couldn't have slowed to a stop in time.

He slid into the hangar, *backward*, and crashed into a rock wall.

He watched in horror as Aya, one tire shy of a full set, clipped the rock face at full speed. Her detached wheel bounced off the far wall and came back at her, glanced off the canopy, and finally disappeared behind her. She flipped and skidded down the corridor upside down, hammering into him.

Event Horizon's seat released Mace from its grip. He threw open the shattered canopy and jumped to the ground. What had he just done?

Aya stirred, still hidden from view. Her canopy ejected open. The force of it righted the vehicle. It teetered for a second, then slammed down, upright. Aya emerged, favoring one side. Her suit was torn open, her forearm bleeding from a gash.

"You maniac!" she screamed at him.

Mace didn't budge. *Don't cry,* he warned himself. *Don't you do it.*

He mustered his courage, taking several long breaths. Ahmed and Raymond appeared in the bay at a sprint, screeching to a halt in front of him, holding large fire extinguishers at the ready. "Are you okay?" Ahmed demanded.

"No. She's—" the word caught in his throat. He pointed at Aya. They noticed her behind him and ran over to her.

"Is she okay?" Mace asked.

Aya had been ready to save his life, and he'd betrayed her. For what?

For everything. To be a TURBOnaut. She would understand. Right?

Hitting your opponents hard is how you're going to win.

"I'll live," he heard her tell Ahmed and Raymond. "Probably need stitches. No. I don't think anything's broken."

Mace approached hesitantly. "I'm so sorry," he begged her.

Don't be sorry.

The blood. It seemed like it was everywhere.

"Apology not accepted, psychopath," she seethed.

Mace shook his head.

Henryk entered the bay, his craft spotless and gleaming. Dex was right behind him.

"Oh, no," muttered Mace. Dex was last. This nightmare was getting worse and worse.

Tempest entered the bay, expressionless. She studied the extensive damage to *Event Horizon* and the dicer.

Ahmed was holding Aya's arm above her heart, tightly wrapping the gash. Raymond gripped a fire extinguisher, at the ready. Aya looked angry, but at least she was alive. Henryk was visibly relieved. Dex's face was made out of stone.

"What in the name of Valhalla happened here?" Henryk demanded.

Tempest strode over to Mace. "You think a stunt like that'll make you a winner?"

"Stunt?" Henryk's eyebrow arched. "He cheated again? I knew it."

"He sure did," Aya fumed.

"No," Mace argued. "Wait."

"No way," Aya shook her head. "You tricked me. I was winning fair and square. You had to cheat to come out on top."

"See what it feels like?" said Henryk. "Told you so."

"Cheating is exactly what you did to me," Dex pointed angrily at Henryk. "You used something. In the water. My dash went on the fritz as you passed me by."

"Prove it," scoffed Henryk.

"Dex, you're done," Tempest interrupted. "Pack your bags."

"No! I swear," he pleaded. "He—"

"Blah, blah blah!" Henryk spat.

"Stop squabbling," Tempest bellowed. "Dex, you finished fourth. You already had a strike. It's over."

Dex stormed out of the bay. Mace watched him go, feeling terrible. He was worried he'd be joining his friend any second.

Tempest watched Dex go, still as a statue.

Finally, she said, "You've put *Event Horizon* out of commission. That's a shame. Heck of a way to retire a legend. Pack your bags."

Mace felt a sudden, hot wave of electricity course through his nerves. "I did what you wanted!" he yelled.

Aya frowned when she heard that. But it was only a brief flicker of confusion, and it vanished.

"All three of you pack your bags." Tempest smiled. "You're going to the Philippines."

"Seriously?" shouted Henryk. "Even Mace?"

Relief washed over Mace. But something else tightened in his stomach. He could have killed Aya. Nothing was worth that risk.

Aya wrenched her arm back from Ahmed. "This is nuts. I'm quitting."

"No." Tempest told her. "Hold on. I'll get you a new dicer. You were amazing out there. We're going to prove dicers are competitive, you and I."

Aya's eyes narrowed, but she stayed silent.

Tempest turned to Henryk. "You were pathetic tonight. You're timid behind a real wheel. It's a good thing you knew how to neutralize Dex, isn't it?"

Henryk's face turned red to match his tousled hair. Mace wasn't sure whether it was fury rising into his cheeks or utter embarrassment.

"I was off tonight," Henryk admitted. "It won't happen again." He looked up. Mace saw a dark, ravenous resolve come over the Norwegian's face. "I'm better than that. I'll win in the Philippines—or die trying."

The scary thing was—Mace believed him.

The others exited the bay. "Aya! Hey, wait. I can explain," Mace called out.

"Explain it to the mountain," she snapped. "You fooled me once, but never again."

What a nightmare. *Event Horizon* was history. He'd totaled a priceless legend. Dex was gone. Aya hated him—and Henryk was clearly out for blood.

And then he wondered: *When is this going to start being fun?*

////// CHAPTER EIGHTEEN

The week leading up to the Philippines Cross-Country TURBO Amateur Showcase was a serious drag. Mace wasn't looking forward to saying goodbye to Dex, who remained at the facility for several days, waiting to catch a bus. Tempest had offered him a ticket home, but Dex wanted to visit relatives in Tucson while he was out west.

Mace wasn't feeling well. The tightness in his gut varied constantly from queasy to run-for-the-bathroom. He'd beaten Aya to the finish line, but his stunt had cost her nine stitches. The way she had clipped the rock face replayed in his mind over and over again. He easily could have ended her life.

Only Dex would talk to him, but they only saw each other during morning meals. Dex's schedule had transitioned back to daytime.

"Got a good feel for her yet?" Dex asked Mace when they were the only two left in the dining room. His suitcase was propped beside him. Soon after Mace went to bed for the day, Dex would depart for the nearest bus station, in the town of Kayenta.

He was referring to Mace's new TURBO racer. It used to be Aya's vehicle, before she switched to the dicer. Mace's new ride was a copy of the original *Event Horizon*, but the differences were real. It was too streamlined, too smooth. It had extra compartments, and Mace suspected their purpose was to hide traps. He could pilot it well enough. But like a jockey on a stranger's horse, they often didn't get along. "I miss my old beast," Mace answered. "I knew her every twitch. I should have gone easier on her."

"Did Tempest send it to the scrap yard yet?" said Dex.

"She said so, but I hope not. I'll convince her to fix it. Could make the difference when it comes to winning the Glove."

"Maybe I'll use my payout to buy it," Dex warned. "Show up in the Philippines, anyway. Caballero, pilot of *Wild Stallion*."

It was clear he was joking, but Mace had to ask, "Did she really pay you enough cash for something like that?"

Dex winked at him. "Just about."

"Wow. Well, I'm not so sad for you anymore."

"Hey, Tempest bought my silence. It's enough money that I'd be stupid to lose it. But I'd rather be in your shoes."

"What're you going to spend it on?" Mace asked.

Dex shrugged. "Cool boots and a cowboy hat. I'm still Caballero, after all. I ought to dress the part. I'll figure the rest out with my sister when I get back to New York. Maybe we'll go back to the D.R."

"You never told me much about your sister," Mace said.

"You never asked. Not much to say. She's a twerp. We're different. But she's still my sis. What about you?" asked Dex. "You don't say much about home, either."

Mace shrugged. "I don't know." He continued, though, sensing that Dex wouldn't make fun of him. "My parents are both deaf."

Dex cast him a curious glance. "Deaf parents? You know sign language?"

"Yup." *Please don't ask me to demonstrate.*

"All right. Cool."

Mace frowned. "You think so?"

"Well, I mean, not like, 'Awesome about your parents!' I bet it's hard. But it's neat that you guys got your own groove. And, you're bilingual. Like the rest of us!"

"I guess so."

"Of course you are." Dex shrugged. "I heard there's a difference, right, between being small-d deaf, or big-D Deaf? What's that about?"

"Yeah," Mace answered. "Small-d deaf is a general term for defining hearing loss. Also, people who can't hear but interact regularly with people who can usually go with the small-d label. Big-D Deaf is like my dad." Mace's dad never used his voice when he signed, and he wanted nothing to do with technology or devices that could give him hearing. "Being Deaf is *who* he is, not *what* he is. He's proud of who he is. And my mom is pretty much the same, but she was born hearing, so she has one foot in each world. Sort of maybe like how Aya is both Japanese and American."

"I told her you want to apologize," Dex said to Mace, like

he could read his mind. "She's still fuming, but she'll come around. She knows Tempest put you up to it. She knows you're a good guy."

Am I? he thought. *I lied to Aya in order to win.*

I buried her.

Made him wonder, *Am I a small-c cheater, or a big-C Cheater?*

He asked Dex, "Did Henryk really do something to you in the water?"

Dex's eyes narrowed at the memory. "I think so. It was weird. I lost power right when he shot by me. But I can't prove it, so, what can I do?"

"I knew he was a skunk," muttered Mace.

"Yeah, well. You're not exactly in a position to complain."

Mace slumped in his seat.

Ahmed entered the dining room. "Time to head out," he told Dex.

The two boys rose and shared a buddy handshake. "Good luck, Mace," Dex said. "I'm rooting for Aya, too. But just be sure one of you creams that guy, okay?"

"You got it," answered Mace. "Maybe someday you can show me the Dominican Republic."

"That'd be fun. And you can show me Colorado."

He watched Dex haul his suitcase out of the room, wondering if he'd ever see his friend again.

//////////////////////////

On the day they were leaving for the Philippines, the knot in Mace's belly went from a bad shoelace job to that thing that happens when you stuff your earbuds into a pocket.

That morning, Tempest took Mace aside at the airport to give him a sneak peak at his new TURBO racer. His vehicle was folded into submersible form.

The sub had a modified shape to it, including new fins and contours. A white *88* was painted on the nose.

Mace pressed his palm into the metal hull, feeling, listening. He moved his hand upward, toward the cockpit, questing. Then he pinpointed it. The ridgeline, which was a couple inches higher than before, emanated a distinct thrum of energy.

"We made a battery mod. Along the dorsal line."

"Battery? There?" he asked, discreetly glancing upward.

"Why don't you jump in the cockpit? There's more to it you need to be aware of."

Mace nestled himself into his seat, and gave the steering

wheel a tight grab. He could feel the adrenaline rushing through his core, as if a race were minutes away. "You're going to fix *Event Horizon,* right?" he asked Tempest.

"No," she told him. "It's time to move this sport forward, Mace. My new models can carry more surprises—more ways to guarantee a win."

"I'm playing by the rules from here on out. Aya—that was too close . . ."

Tempest took a deep breath. "Do you want to wear that Glove, or not?"

Mace didn't say anything.

"You see this button?" She pointed to something under the dash.

Mace crouched in the cockpit as well as he could. He found it. There was a new button beneath the steering column. "What is it? Something to do with the dorsal battery?"

Tempest gave a single nod.

"What does it do?"

Tempest's good eye studied him closely. "You should be smart enough by now to know when to stop asking questions."

Mace was silent for a long time. "I don't need to cheat to win."

Tempest pursed her lips. "Who said anything about cheating? You know how the surface area of a tennis racket has more than doubled since tennis's early days?"

"Um . . . sure."

"It's because someone realized that there was no rule saying you couldn't use a bigger racket. And they won with it. Was that cheating? Or vision? What we're doing is engineering bigger, better tennis rackets. We're ushering the sport into a new—and more lucrative—age."

"Well, let's go all the way, then," Mace joked. "Laser cannons. That would guarantee a win."

"Yes, true." She laughed. "But that's clearly against the rules, and you'd never get away with it."

Mace stared at her. "So this is about what we can get away with?"

"When is it not?"

Mace laughed but stopped abruptly when he realized she wasn't joking.

"The winners in this crazy world are the ones who see

the holes in the rules. And I'm going to make a fortune setting the trend. Just think about it. After we win this year, teams will buy up my vehicles, my innovations. They'll get ahead. I'll sell even more innovations. Then before we know it, audiences will be screaming for the excitement of new ways to duel on the track. Suddenly, pulse beams and deflector shields will be normal. And the name Hollande will have cornered the market! My logo will be on every TURBO racer."

"We're trailblazers, eh?"

"If no one's blazing trails, Mace, the world has nowhere to go."

Mace wasn't buying it, though. *Blazing trails?* Success through any means necessary didn't feel like breaking new ground. It didn't feel like an exciting business opportunity, either. If he was being honest with himself, it felt like cheating. And as far as big ideas go, cheating to win wasn't only a well-worn path, it was older than dirt.

CHAPTER NINETEEN //////

Mace always knew traveling outside the United States would feel exotic. But when he glanced around Manila, he felt overwhelmed by the congested, brightly lit city. Wide boulevards lined with glass skyscrapers intermixed with small brick buildings. New skyscrapers were under construction everywhere, crowned with swinging cranes. Walking down a crowded alleyway, Mace marveled at road signs and storefront banners in English and Tagalog. He had to duck sagging power lines, he nearly tripped over a live chicken that had escaped a roadside vendor, and he snagged his shirt on rebar sticking straight out the side of a concrete building.

Henryk's red hair was matted down and damp. Dirty sweat streaked down his face. He was hanging close to Tempest and Ahmed as their group tried to catch a ride. Henryk's eyes darted this way and that, like cliff swallows hunting bugs. When a street vendor jumped out to offer him a hat that was also an umbrella, Henryk yelped.

Aya and Mace laughed at the same time. Then Aya seemed to remember that she was supposed to hate Mace. She frowned. He looked down at her forearm, wrapped from wrist to elbow with a long, rectangular bandage. Nine stitches there. A gnarly scar would remain on her arm for the rest of her life. A TURBO souvenir, courtesy of Mace Blazer.

"Get a good look," Tempest told them. "Next time you see this street, you'll be zooming by at triple-digit speeds. Here's our ride. Hop on."

They piled into a waiting jeepney. Half mini school bus, half jeep, this was public transportation in the Philippines. They were off to grab a peek at tomorrow morning's starting line. Mace watched Henryk carefully. He seemed to snap out of a trance when Tempest mentioned the word "speed."

Mace could see that Henryk was suddenly focused.

Henryk was going to be fierce tomorrow. *Win or die trying.* Mace would have to match that attitude. This was the last competition. Only one of them would go on from here.

The jeepney carrying their group was airbrushed every color of the rainbow. Wooden banners hung on its sides: *GOD KNOWS HUDAS NOT PAY, BOODLE FIGHT!, DRIVER NOT LIABLE FOR ANYTHING.* A plastic Jesus blinked like a Christmas light above the driver's bald head. The driver kept looking up at Mace, flashing him a thumbs-up every few seconds, then jerking the wheel to the left or right to correct his steering. He honked his horn at random intervals, waving to passersby lining the streets.

The group reached the starting-line plaza. Already, several trimorphers were parked, waiting. Security patrols marched about, setting up a wide perimeter. Construction teams were setting up bleachers along the sidewalks.

"You're starting in the last three slots tomorrow. Take a quick look around; make good notes," Tempest announced on board the jeepney. She sported large, dark sunglasses and wore a headscarf. She clearly didn't want anyone to recognize her.

"Tempest, these are trophy toy cars. I could beat any one of them in my sleep," Aya said, taking in the scene on the street. Of the dozen vehicles already set up in line for the start of tomorrow's race, four of them had hoods up, revealing Allied or Mazagatti hybrid-electric engines without so much as a dust mote on them, or Olympus-Niner thermocouples still wrapped in factory plastic. Mace spotted numerous extra gadgets that looked cool and were clearly expensive but might actually hinder performance during flight. He had to squint to fight the spotless shine of their hulls.

Tempest cautioned them. "Don't get the wrong impression. Most of these blowhards are indulging a fantasy, yes. But a few of these guys could've been pros. A few of them used to be pros. They want their glory back. Take nothing for granted."

A stray dog paused at the wheel of a banana-yellow TURBO craft, lifted its leg, and offered its appreciation. A man wearing an unrelenting yellow polo shirt yelled at the mutt, shooing it away. He spun around and scolded the crew. A boy was among the pit crew, leaning against the door of the vehicle. He was laughing, which only made the man more angry.

Mace choked.

The boy was Carson Gerber.

He gave the Gerb and the yellow vehicle behind him a double take. The man in the polo shirt must be Robert Gerber, Carson's dad. Which also made him Mace's mom's boss. Mace watched the Gerbers, fascinated. That yellow, it was . . . Mace couldn't stress this enough—it was the single most vivid color his eyes had ever absorbed. Mr. Gerber stroked his thick brown mustache, carrying himself with pride. He was taking race prep seriously. Carson, on the other hand, reminded Mace of Henryk: full of himself, but with nothing to show for it. The Gerb lifted his leg, mimicking the dog, and his dad became visibly red faced in response.

Mace filed out of the jeepney. Tempest had an arm around Aya. They were looking at a rival dicer, discussing something. Henryk had drifted separately into the plaza, getting close-up looks at the competition. Sensing a window, Mace took a deep breath and marched over to the Gerbers.

"Hey, Carson," Mace said. "So, what do you call this thing? Please don't say *Banana Peel.*"

The Gerb stared, his jaw slowly unhinging. "Mace?" he

finally stammered, slowly rising from the stool he had occupied. "What. Are. You. Doing. Here?"

Mace soaked up the Gerb's display of early-stage heart failure with glee.

Robert Gerber stepped forward. He was on the plump side, with short curly hair to match his mustache. The polo shirt was tight on him and soaked with sweat. His smile was genuine and friendly. "Hi, Mace!" he said. "I was wondering if we'd run into you. How's the internship thing going?"

Mace was caught off guard by the strange twist in the conversation, but not as much as Carson was.

"Internship?" Carson asked his dad.

"He's a TURBO squire," the old man explained to his son. "Got into a summer program." He pivoted to Mace. "Very cool stuff. Who are you crewing for? One of the new teams they just announced? All in black?"

Of course! His mom would have bragged to everyone she knew about her son's "summer scholarship"—especially her boss, who was an obvious TURBO fan. "I'm actually not allowed to say," Mace told Mr. Gerber.

"Ha! Okay. No worries," Mr. Gerber said. "Cloak and dagger. I understand."

"How'd you get an internship with TURBO?" Carson asked him.

Mace grew tight-lipped. No one was supposed to know who he was. It had been a mistake to wander over here, no matter how satisfying it had been to see the Gerb's face melt like a wax statue under a hot lamp. "Oh, you know. Good grades."

"Congratulations, Mace," Mr. Gerber said. "I told your mom I wasn't surprised. I've always been very impressed with you."

"What do you call your racer?" Mace asked, pointing at the otherworldly-yellow TURBO craft. It was respectable-looking if you weren't blinded by its sheer, blinding . . . yellowness. Well cared for, but with enough dings and scratches to suggest Carson's dad wasn't afraid to elbow his way through the pack.

"*Brown Trout*," Robert answered. Mace laughed. But the man wasn't joking. Carson slapped a palm to his forehead, but his father beamed with pride as he spoke. "It's a fly-fishing thing. Brown trout are actually pretty yellow, if you catch the lighting just right. And, plus, my mustache is brown, so there's that connection."

"Dad, stop talking," suggested Carson.

"Brown trout turn their most yellow during spawning season. Anyway, yeah, she's a speedboater. A skimmer. No underwater antics for me. Too dangerous for my tastes."

"Okay," Mace replied. Mace could see Mr. Gerber's love for the sport was legit. There was magic in it for him. Mace knew the feeling. *How could a guy this nice be the father of such a tool?*

"I'm shooting for a win." Mr. Gerber winked. "The top placers tomorrow get a chance to enter the San Fran Pro-Am. That's a big opportunity. If an amateur pilot goes on to place in San Francisco, against the pros, they're automatically entered into a special wild-card Gauntlet Prix spot. Long shot, but what a dream, huh?"

That's interesting, Mace thought. Not his concern, though. Tempest had gone around those channels. She'd already bought her way into a Gauntlet Prix berth. But it was nice to imagine a hobbyist climbing their way to the top, too.

"Tell your pilot to stay out of my way tomorrow, eh?" Robert winked again. "I've got an all-new engine in here. Rolls-Royce Pegasus X-90. Class D. Top of the line."

"Wow," said Mace, genuinely impressed. "That's, like,

honestly the most powerful engine on the market." *What in the world is he doing with that much kick?* marveled Mace. *He's likely to kill himself out there!* "You plan on breaking Earth's orbit?"

"Naw. But I wouldn't be the first civilian to try."

"You trim the thrust performance on that thing, right?" Mace was serious. "Please tell me you do."

"Of course I do!" Robert came clean. "Do I look like I'm crazy?"

Mace kept his mouth shut, but Carson filled the silence. "Dad, you *are* crazy."

Mace took a step back. "I'll, um . . . I'll keep an eye out for you on the road tomorrow," he said.

"All you'll see is a yellow blur." Robert smiled confidently.

Mace imagined what the *Brown Trout* would look like as he blew past the old man somewhere on the highway before they left Manila. *You're absolutely right,* Mace silently agreed.

///// CHAPTER TWENTY

"Please give a warm welcome to Robert 'Fly-Fisher' Gerber, and *Brown Trout*."

The crowds clapped politely somewhere beyond the canvas walls of Tempest's team tent. Introductions of each TURBOnaut were underway and would culminate any moment with the announcement of Mace and the other two late "mystery" entrants.

"*Brown Trout*?" Aya asked the group, hidden away in their waiting area. "Someone named their racer after a *fish*?"

Mace held back a laugh.

"It's an amateur event." Ahmed shrugged. "What do you expect?"

The four of them were huddled around a card table, seated in a tent near the plaza where the race would soon begin. Mace was glad to be hidden. Aya sighed, remembering back. "It's like a kid with a new pet. I had a turtle once. I named it Elephant."

"See?" said Ahmed. "I had a pet rooster named Marilyn Monroe."

"Yeah, but these aren't little kids with dumb pets," Aya argued.

"Sure they are," Henryk fired back. "At least these rich yokels get to name their vehicles," he grumbled. "And paint them."

Tempest had insisted her mentees all remain anonymous during this race. Their helmets would never come off, and they would have no names. She would allow the winner to choose the paint colors, but she would be naming the vehicles and choosing his or her racing names herself. For now, they all were black, and only white numbers—eighty-three and eighty-eight—distinguished the boys' vehicles.

The announcer was moving down the list. "And next we have another retired pro. Welcome Fat Man, pilot of *Radio-active*." The applause continued.

"What would you call your ride?" Mace asked Henryk. "*Dasher*? *Dancer*? *Prancer*? Or *Vixen*?"

"What *will* I call my ride," Henryk corrected. "I've got it all picked out. I'm thinking gold and silver for the colors."

"So, you're going to name her *Bling Bling*?" said Mace.

His eyes met Aya's and caught her smile. He remembered how much he missed her laugh.

"No," stammered Henryk. "It's going to be *Mjölnir*. Thor's hammer."

"That's actually kind of cool," Mace admitted.

"I'd go with *Lotus*," said Aya. "Lavender and green—like a lotus flower on a lake."

"What about you, Mace?" Henryk asked.

He jerked. It was the first time in forever that Henryk had asked him a question. "Um," he started. He'd put a little thought into this, lately, but nothing had come to mind. The racer he was using—it felt like a rental. Temporary. He didn't feel right giving it a name. "I don't have one picked out yet. But I like dark blue and burnt orange as colors, so . . . I dunno."

"And now," the announcer's tinny voice bellowed from unseen loudspeakers out on the street, "introducing our final wild cards in today's amateur showcase."

"That's us," said Aya.

Henryk waltzed passed them, pressing his helmet down on his head as he exited the tent. "Bye, losers. You can say you knew me when."

"Nice," said Mace. "A farewell speech for the ages!"

Aya rose, took a deep breath, and donned her helmet. Her black visor regarded Mace for several seconds. "Come anywhere near me, and I swear, I'll make you regret it."

"I was only following orders," he said.

He wanted to assure her it was true. But at the end of the day, Mace was the one behind the wheel. Cheating had been his call. He owned it—even if he didn't like it. "But I'll never do it again."

"Your words mean nothing to me," Aya said. She stepped out of the tent. After a moment, he followed.

Crowds along the sidewalks, and clustered everywhere along rooftops and balconies, clapped politely for them. It was a lukewarm welcome, but Mace understood. Tempest had kept their identities secret. Why should anyone care about them?

Ahmed escorted them to their vehicles, parked in roadster form at the back of a line of twenty motley trimorphers, arranged in rows of two all the way down the block.

Mace passed Robert "Fly-Fisher" Gerber on his way, who looked up from his final inspection of *Brown Trout* to scrutinize the newcomers.

Ahmed helped secure the straps on Mace's gleaming black helmet and stood back to examine him. His expression was reserved.

"Tempest is already in the air, en route to the finish. But we'll both be on the wire with you every second. Talk to us," he said. "We're your eyes and ears. We'll pick up on things you can't see."

"No danger of being overheard?" Mace asked.

"Nope. All signals are encrypted. Our comms are private. But keep the chatter down anyway, because your vehicle records every transmission. It comes in handy for reviewing performance afterward."

Mace sighed. "Can I ask you something, Ahmed?"

The engineer set down his clipboard. "Anything."

"Why is winning the Gauntlet Prix so important to Tempest? She keeps talking about using the sport to get rich. But she's already got tons of money."

Ahmed didn't answer right away. He helped Mace into the cockpit and leaned in to reach the dash himself. He flipped a series of switches in sequence, going over a prerace checklist. "People can have everything," he began, "and still never have enough." Ahmed grew serious, searching Mace closely. "But you know better. You race because you love the sport. You race for you."

"Well, yeah," Mace confirmed. He thought of that feeling he got every time the engine fired up. It was close to pure joy.

"Good," said Ahmed. He wiped his greasy hands clean on a white shop cloth pinned to his belt. "Then it's worth it."

Ahmed scurried away to help Aya with her final prep. Tempest appeared to Mace over a live video feed on one of his displays. Her black eye patch loomed large as she leaned in close to the camera. He could see her private jet's lounge surrounding her.

"Watch your entries. Remember, you only get three pit stops. In and out. Keep your touchdowns smooth. It's a long run. Don't blow your shocks early."

"Understood," Mace said.

"Understood?" she mocked. "What's going on, Mace? Where's your adrenaline? Henryk is so amped he's just about yanking his steering wheel from the socket. Aya looks like a soldier going to war. But you . . . I don't know."

"Don't worry about me," Mace said.

"You stay on the radio, you hear?" she told him. "This is a cakewalk. If you can't win this, you don't stand a chance at the Gauntlet. Still, we have a 'Golden' opportunity today to practice a few things." She winked at him with her one good eye.

Mace's stomach did a flip. He looked away, fidgeted with a dial. The canopy began to close.

"Mace. Listen to me," she said. "My father always told me: you either take a seat at the table, or you're on the menu."

She lifted her eye patch and tilted her rotten grape of an eye in his direction.

Surprised, Mace looked away.

"When I was young, I was like you. I was idealistic. My reward: I was sabotaged. They ripped my life out from under my feet that day. I vowed after that to always be the first to strike."

"Who's 'they'?" he asked.

"Who do you think could pull off something like what happened?" she asked as if the answer were obvious.

"You mean, the TURBO Association?" He frowned.

She readjusted the patch over her eye. "It's the only possible explanation."

"Wait." Mace had seen the footage from that fateful race. No one had been near her on that last lap. She'd been sailing ahead of the pack. She'd slowed down, seemingly on purpose. But *why?* Had her foot slipped? Nerves? Was she trying to spring a trap even back then? "That doesn't . . ."

Everything started to click into place. His mind raced.

He suddenly realized she'd spent a lifetime denying that crash was her own fault. She was convinced everyone cheats because it was the only way she could explain what happened without blaming herself.

Tempest's head snapped up. She glowered at him. "It's the truth. Like it or not."

"But—" Mace never finished his thought. The announcer's bold voice came through the cockpit's closed-circuit radio loud and clear. "Ladies and gentlemen, start your engines!"

A monstrous roar reverberated through the airtight cockpit, accompanied by an awesome rattling in Mace's rib cage. The trimorphers ahead of him in line fired up, thousands of pistons building power in magnificent, tectonic concert. Last in line, Mace was on the receiving end of a volcanic churning of horsepower, twenty racers throttling up for the start of the cross-country showcase.

Mace's finger hovered over the ignition. He noticed his hands were shaking. "Keep it cool, pal. You've got this. Nice and smooth." He clenched his fists, and when he re-extended the fingers, they were steady as stones.

Tempest remained front and center on his video display. Mace held her angry gaze. "Stay in touch," she warned him. "You know what I'm talking about."

He tapped the screen. "You're breaking up. Sorry!"

"You're pushing my buttons, Mace," she scolded. "When the time comes, you better make sure you push the right ones."

////// CHAPTER TWENTY-ONE

Red light. Yellow light. Green light. Tires peeled. Smoke bellowed. The cityscape blurred.

A full-terrain race. The course was one route—a straight shot from Manila, seven hundred kilometers south to the island of Mindanao, in and out of the water as the TURBO-nauts hopped from island to island.

Mace had forgotten his vehicle's kick. He nearly rear-ended Henryk coming off the starting line. He corrected too forcefully, hitting the brakes. Rookie mistake. Mace felt his face grow warm, and he cursed under his breath.

Struggling in dead last place. It just wasn't the same without that antique at his command. *Doesn't matter. Get in there. Introduce yourself!*

Henryk and Aya were already breaking ahead, banking into the first curve of the billboard-lined highway. The squadron of roadsters directly in front of Mace lurched forward.

Mace gunned it, eager to stay on them.

"All right, Mace. You've crossed the start line." Tempest spoke in his ears. "You're a TURBOnaut. Congratulations. Now you better move it unless you want to be the last 'naut to enter the bay. There's a gap between *Unicorn* and *Radioactive*. Strike right up the middle of it."

Mace saw what she was talking about. The curve eased up, giving him an opening. He leaned forward and unleashed his vehicle's full fury. His gut swelled; his grip tightened on the wheel. Mace whipped to the right, punched the pedal, and took *Radioactive* on the inside curve of the highway. He rocketed by the rainbow-colored *Unicorn* and two more novices and entered the next turn tight on the inside lane, gaining ground for another series of passes.

Somehow, *Radioactive* had crept back up on him. Fat Man tried to shoot past, but Mace pinned him against the highway wall, and he backed off. The next curve belonged to Mace, and he pressed his advantage, stealing the lead on the inside.

That guy used to be a pro. I'm doing good here!

He let out a war cry, which quickly turned into a grunt of alarm.

A clunky-looking rust-colored roadster came out of nowhere, shooting the gap between Mace and *Radioactive*. Mace let the junker go by. Its pilot was clearly in over his head. Nothing to worry about.

"Ground-to-water entry in T minus twenty seconds," Tempest advised.

The highway lifted high above the sprawling city below. Mace gave it some gas, passed several more roadsters. He retook the rusty roadster as the end of the road was coming up. Mace spotted *Brown Trout* zigging and zagging on the water's surface, dueling other speedboaters. Mace grinned. Dude had talent.

Henryk and Aya both dropped out of view in front of him, and he caught a quick glimpse of their roadsters morphing into submersibles before he lost them from view.

He entered behind them a second later. Manila Bay was

murky. Tempest had warned him about this, but it still came as a shock. Mace could sometimes see only as far as the cockpit glass. He trusted his detectors and his own senses. Aya was not far ahead. Her trajectory was pulling her wide of the first ring. Mace maintained a straight route, sensing the ring directly ahead. He passed Aya, shot through the ring, and found himself near enough to the tail of a craft to read its name: *Leviathan*.

On the water's surface, speedboaters tacked along a wider course that accounted for their advantage in speed and visibility. Who was actually in the lead? Mace couldn't quite say.

Below the surface, he felt out the route. He hit every ring without seeing them. He advanced on two speedboaters swerving broadly around buoys. One of them had a bright-yellow belly like the sun shining down on the ocean. Mr. Gerber.

The water was filled with old industrial fishing nets drifting through the currents. Mace dodged them, losing time, but hopeful a rival would get caught and make the maneuver worth it.

Sure enough, Tempest reported that *Code Talker* and

Demigod had each been netted, taking them out of the running. Mace overtook *Leviathan* during the confusion. Then one of the skimmers caught a steel cable in its propeller. Mace glanced up. *Brown Trout* was still in the running.

Ahmed chimed in. "Get ready to air-morph. You're going to fly over all of Mindoro and touch down on the coastal highway of Panay. That's a winding sixty miles before a quick air jump to Cadiz City. We'll see you there for a pit stop."

Mace shot airborne, momentarily distracted by the scenery. The islands were gorgeous! Sheer, limestone cliff faces, wave-wracked, rose hundreds of feet above dark green jungles.

He regained his focus. Hurry. Faster. The compulsion to skirt the edge of disaster, to thumb his nose at physics, was strong.

Carson's dad had a fast aircraft, but he was a fish out of water behind the controls. "Top-of-the-line Rolls-Royce Pegasus, say hello to my smart-cushioned buttocks." Mace inched up on him. The old man had no idea how to box Mace out. He passed *Brown Trout* with a barrel roll and never looked back.

Mace searched the sky for Henryk, finally catching sight of him. He dropped into Henryk's wake. This was a long race. There was plenty of time.

The Norwegian wanted this win. Too bad Mace wasn't going to let that happen. He took the lead when Henryk botched an air-to-ground morph.

But it wasn't meant to last. On the curving roads of Panay Henryk flung past him.

Mace growled. He couldn't believe Henryk was drifting on these roads. Vertical cliffs. Crumbling pavement. He was on a suicide mission.

"I thought you were my guy," Tempest said as Aya outmaneuvered Mace on the next steep curve, swinging into the turns with her tail arcing wide.

Mace held his breath, accelerated into the next sharp turn. He shifted into second gear and then held down the clutch with his foot.

"Okay," he told himself. "Just remember, you *do* have wings, if it comes to that. . . ." But he wasn't finding the thought very reassuring. Wings were pretty useless in a tumbling free fall.

He flicked the steering wheel in the direction of his turn and ripped the hand brake. As Mace hugged the edge of the road, the ocean suddenly loomed large and vast to one side of his canopy.

Mace closed his eyes.

He felt the engine torque. Instinct kicked in, and he was able to harness the knock of extra momentum.

He pried his eyes open and risked a glance down at the water. That sense of vertigo morphed into exhilaration as he made the turn. He gunned it into the straightaway. With the wheels locked, he kicked it into high gear and exploded down the next switchback.

He gave a squeal of pent-up delight.

Aya fishtailed wide around the following sharp turn, cutting into a straight shot without losing speed. Mace despaired. How would he pass her? Drifting was one thing, but drifting around someone else who was also drifting? And on such a tight road?

They wound down off the cliffs and took to the water again, where Mace continued to lose in the standings. But once he shot airborne, he quickly gained back lost ground.

The lead changed constantly from island to island. Aya usually came out ahead when their tracks met back up. She kept besting him in the air. Mace had to wonder if the dicer course was fair.

"I can't tell who's in the lead!" Mace complained.

"Push your own limits," warned Tempest. "The standings will sort themselves out."

The end was in sight: a checkered banner a mile down the main drag of Cagayan de Oro, on the north coast of Mindanao. But first, one last hoop checkpoint in the air a half mile off the coast. Mace had fallen behind Henryk and Aya after another series of missteps on the winding cliffside roads of Cebu. Aya was on a beeline run toward the hoop as Mace and Henryk merged in from the left. But the black twins, TURBO racers *88* and *83*, were screaming bullets, with more speed in reserve. It was clear to Mace already that he and Henryk would beat the dicer to the ground.

She had done more with a dicer than anyone ever had before.

But she would place behind the boys all the same.

Aya. Out. *No hard feelings,* he hoped.

"Take him from below," ordered Tempest. "Get up on him! Take him."

Mace obeyed, seeing the strategy clearly. It would be tight, but he thought he could beat Henryk to the hoop. He dipped and picked up speed, feeling the g-forces pressing his spine into the smart cushioning.

Mace pulled up below Henryk with seconds to spare.

"Push the button, Mace."

Mace gulped in surprise. "I don't need to, Tempest!"

"PUSH THE BUTTON!"

"I DON'T NEED TO!" He inched past Henryk and took the position. The TURBOnauts came in for a hard landing, touching off the final ground stretch toward the checkered flag.

His rear displays flashed. Henryk was right on his tail, and Aya was right behind Henryk.

"MACE! I gave you an order. Take them out!"

He corrected to the left, cutting off Aya. But Henryk was coming in fast, again, nosing up on him. The checkered flag was right there.

"Last chance, Mace." Tempest's voice was cool. "Striking first is your best defense."

What does that mean?

Mace shut off the radio. He hammered the pedal, toggled his thrusters. "Come on, baby. Come on!"

There was a jolt in the engine. Mace's craft veered unexpectedly! He lost ground. Henryk was suddenly ahead of him!

Not possible!

Mace roared with anger. He knew in a flash: An energy deflector! Henryk had used a secret booby trap on *him*.

It must have been exactly what he'd done to Dex.

Doesn't matter. I can recover. Mace gunned it. The flag. It was coming . . . then gone. Mace glanced to his side. Henryk was right there, his featureless visor glancing back at him through the glare of his canopy.

He flipped on the radio. An acid silence met his ears. "Who took it?" Mace demanded. No response. His heart was in his chest. He slowed into the next turn with a deep dread settling in. "Tell me!"

A crackle came. "Stand by, Mace." It was Ahmed. His voice sounded grim.

"What's going on?"

"It's a photo finish."

"A photo finish?" gasped Mace.

Mace slowed, coming up on the pit ramp. Henryk stayed

on his shoulder. The winner always enters the pits first. But Henryk wouldn't back off to let Mace go ahead.

I won this, Mace wanted to scream at Henryk. *And I did it even after you sabotaged me.* "Back off!"

The crowds in the bleachers were still as statues. Mace glanced at the megascreens. Their nose-to-nose finish was on constant replay. It was hard to tell. . . . Every angle showed a dead tie. The images zoomed in. Computer graphics analyzed their positions. Suddenly, the crowds erupted. He stole a glance back up.

Mace's number, *88*, was flashing on all the screens.

He had taken first.

And he'd done it in spite of Henryk's treachery.

He screamed his joy.

"What are you so happy about?" Tempest asked him.

"I won!" he said. "I told you I could do it no matter what. I'm going to the Gauntlet Prix!"

He was met with silence. It lasted a full beat—an eternity to Mace. When Tempest next spoke, her voice was harsh. "No, you're not," she said. "I'm advancing Henryk."

"What? No!" he said. "You can't do that!"

"Yes, I can. I own you. I decide!" she came back.

Mace felt his stomach plummet. "I'll take my helmet off when we park. I'll tell the world what you're doing, cheating at every turn."

"Oh, really? You wanna know something? I got a call from the cops the other day. They had some follow-ups about the theft of the *Event Horizon*. They were asking some interesting questions."

"What does that have to do with anything?"

"You tell me," she spat. "Or have you forgotten that you broke into a highly restricted facility with your father's help and stole a museum exhibit? Would be a shame if the Feds eventually tracked that night's events back to you. Back to your *dad*. Don't you think?"

Mace gripped the steering wheel. His heart rate was off the charts. "You leave my dad out of this!"

"Then follow orders for once!" Tempest bellowed in his ears. "You were given a job to do. You failed. I warned you what was a stake."

"I won."

"I don't care."

"I'm better than Henryk—"

"I. Don't. Care. Henryk does what I tell him to. You really

think you'd have a prayer against the pros in the Gauntlet League? You don't have the guts to revolutionize this sport, Mace. You lost in all the important ways—and now guess what? You're on the menu instead of sitting at the table. It's time for you to shut up and go home."

TWO WEEKS LATER

CHAPTER TWENTY-TWO /////

You're on the menu instead of sitting at the table.

Golden arcade tokens dropped from a dispenser into a metal dish, and one fell to the trampled carpet. Mace, several feet away, heard it roll unnoticed beneath the token machine. There was a time, not too long ago, when he would have hurried over to the coin changer and crouched down to fish underneath it for the freebie. Not today.

"Take me out to the ball game!" trumpeted over the din of the arcade. Mace could hear swooshing ninja kicks connecting with bad-guy foreheads. Grubby hands pounded sticky buttons. A machine gun mowed through an army of zombie alien insects. The overhead speakers competed for attention with a muffled, "Michael, your chili dog is ready. Michael. Chili dog!"

Mace wandered the game-room aisles, searching for something to play. But nothing appealed. His ears zeroed in on a flipper bat striking a pinball. The ball sailed through a tunnel, racking up thousands of pointless points.

Behind him, at the center of the arcade, the hydraulic joints of robotic stick legs flexed and released, rose and fell, rotating a featureless white pod.

But Mace refused to pay attention to that. He wouldn't bring himself to look at the Hollande Industries TURBO simulator. He just couldn't . . . .

Why had he come to the mall? How had he fooled himself into believing this would work?

He was trying to salvage what was left of his summer. He used to escape here. He used to lose himself in the stormy sea of beeping and bopping and clanking and tinny, eight-bit jingles, the *pew-pew!* of spaceships firing lasers, the smell of popcorn, burnt nachos, and pink bubble gum.

But the chaos no longer comforted him like it used to.

Mace had thought maybe that by getting into the simulator, he could begin to let go of the fantasy that he could have been more. But as soon as he arrived, he was haunted by the possibility that the machine would recognize him somehow. Tempest and Ahmed would know that he had returned like a dog with its tail between its legs.

He turned. He lifted his eyes and watched the simulator dance upon its pedestals. It moved so gracefully, dipping and soaring, veering. It rattled at times, but on purpose. Mace could imagine the aircraft jouncing down on asphalt, passing another vehicle, shifting into a different gear. The virtual pod came very close to replicating the authentic feel of every moment in a real race.

But it was all a lie.

And that was the thing. The whole past month had been a lie. What Tempest had been offering all along was little more than a way to cheat.

He only wanted to race—and to earn the respect of his heroes along the way.

"If I had to do it all over again, I'd do it again exactly the same," he said out loud.

He couldn't watch the news, or his favorite sports shows.

He'd never be able to watch a TURBO race again. Too painful.

And he'd missed attending his mechanical engineering camp to boot.

He circled the simulator, coming around to the side of the boarding platform. The employee stationed there gave him a nod, recognizing him. Mace smiled back and kept circling. The simulator bucked. Mace guessed whoever was inside had just morphed from water to air.

Monitors beyond the boarding platform looped rapid-fire ads for the simulator, the imagery cut from terrain to terrain, vehicle to vehicle, showcasing highlights from historical Gauntlets Prix.

Iron Dragon, burnt red and smoky black, swooped across a forest glade. A video game Talon waved at the screen, his pixilated likeness a bit off but recognizable. Talon was known for his well-groomed blond goatee and spiky blond hair with fiery-red tips. *You'll never look that cool,* Mace daydreamed telling Henryk.

He imagined Henryk's whiskery face selling this game to a new generation of avid TURBO fans and wanted to puke.

The usual sound effects cut out. The screen flickered, transitioning to a replay of a real *TURBOWORLD* sportscast.

Wearing a trademark American-flag tie and a shiny blue blazer, star commentator Jax Anders reported the latest TURBO news from his glass desk. The studio cut away to grainy, spectator footage of . . . Mace's finish-line duel with Henryk!

Mace drew closer.

The twin black trimorphers were a confusing blur against a shifting coastal island backdrop.

It looks so glamorous, but it's all a sham.

Mace had gone to great lengths to avoid the buzz created by that photo finish. Seeing himself on TV for the first time, he was equal parts amused and brokenhearted.

As if in a trance, he leaned in to hear what the famed announcer had to say.

"Welcome, TURBO maniacs, to your daily dose of all things TURBO. Confirmed just this afternoon: the mystery black-clad pilot of trimorpher *88,* who took the world of TURBO by storm a fortnight ago, *will* participate in next month's Gauntlet Prix, spanning from Mexico City to Miami over the course of two grueling days."

That's me! I was piloting 88*!* Mace wanted to scream.

"To celebrate the announcement, TURBO's newest

sensation finally has a name. The pilot will answer to the call of Infinity. How about that? I'm told the moniker is in reference to his double eights. And he's got a new look! Check out that sleek gold-and-silver design, maniacs! They've christened this elegant chariot *Continuum*."

Mace couldn't help but be impressed by the polished *Continuum* on display. Its silver-and-gold knot work was spectacular. If Mace didn't know any better, he would be fawning all over the design, along with the rest of the world.

Instead, clenching his fists, he was seized by jealousy. He repeated aloud this time: "I'm number 88. That was me!"

Jax Anders, on the other side of the television glass, wasn't interested in Mace's tell-all confession. "And what's the latest from the other two mystery morphers, you ask? We've got the scoop, maniacs. We'll get back to the dicer pilot in a moment. For now, I want to personally weigh in on the theory that the pilot of black craft *83* employed some sort of black-magic stealth jammer. Look how *Continuum* gets ramrodded, here. There was no physical contact. Foul play? Sure looks like it."

"No," said Mace. He was vaguely aware that his teeth

hurt, and he loosened his jaw. "This isn't happening."

"What's more is it turns out *Continuum*'s handler is none other than the billionaire heiress, Tempest Hollande. The telecommunications giant was mobbed coming down the steps of TURBO Association headquarters earlier today after the news broke."

Anders's face disappeared, replaced by a scene of reporters crowded around Tempest. A bunch of mics were shoved in her face.

"Why did you designate Infinity as a cryptic?" a reporter asked her.

"Infinity has reasons for entering the sport in a mask. You'll get your answer soon enough, I promise," Tempest said. Her bejeweled eye patch caught a flash of sunlight and sparkled. It covered most of the scarring around her eye, but not quite all of it. Her neck burns were hidden behind a fashionable high collar.

"What can you say to critics and skeptics, Ms. Hollande, to convince them that this isn't just a publicity stunt for another one of your new lines of products?"

"My 'naut will answer the skeptics by winning the Glove.

Until then, I'll leave you with this: If you know me at all, you know I love to make a splash. I'd get ready to get wet, folks! Thank you."

She forcibly steered away from the mob. The reporters took this as a cue to start screaming more questions, twice as fast, twice as loud.

"Which of your shell companies is funding your new hobby, Ms. Hollande?"

"Who built *Continuum*? Why doesn't your team have any outside sponsors?"

The video toggled back to *TURBOWORLD*. Jax Anders was behind his desk, speaking to former TURBOnaut Rex Danger, retired pilot of *Triassic*. They were discussing the history of "cryptics" in the sport. Danger had begun his own career as a masked wild card entrant. Mystery pilots had always been an aspect of the sport, though they were rare, and no serious cryptics had come forward in the past several years. "Most of it comes down to ratings and attention," Danger explained. "A little mystery's good for business. It's that simple."

"Thank you, Rex, for that insight." Jax pivoted back to the camera. "Speaking of stellar performances, I told you we'd return to the subject of that dicer pilot seen in the Philippines alongside *Continuum*. The hotshot with death-defying skills has become such a fan favorite, Tempest Hollande has decided to sponsor a slot in late July's San Fran Pro-Am. She's registered the name *Lotus* for the vehicle. As for me, thank you for asking, I'm looking forward to seeing more sensational performances out of *Lotus* and her mystery 'naut, Katana. Together, they've renewed tons of interest in both dicers and skimmers as legitimate competitors in the premiere league. And I think that's a positive development."

Mace took several steps back. "Aya."

She gets to keep racing. Good for her.

But then it dawned on him: *Tempest chose two pilots.* He felt alone. The news seemed to double the weight of his own failure.

Aya. He never had a chance to talk to her after the race. Tempest had hustled him onto the first flight back to the US.

Mace had figured he could look Aya up at some point. But now that she was a real TURBOnaut, he worried he'd never get the chance.

Mace turned away from the *TURBOWORLD* rebroadcast,

ready to skulk out of the arcade, out of the mall, maybe into oncoming traffic. The gulf between what he could have had and what he was now left with felt impossibly vast.

The simulator in the corner grew still, returned to the off position. Mace noticed the quiet that came over the entire arcade. He glanced up at the opaque hatch and stopped short.

A dude with an expensive-looking cowboy hat and shiny leather boots stepped out of the pod.

Mace laughed.

Dex's eyes immediately snagged on Mace, and he gave his friend an intentional, wry grin and a tip of the hat. He strode down the boarding platform steps and met Mace on the game-room floor.

"What is this?" Mace slapped his brown leather vest. "Where's your sheriff's badge?"

Dex let his Spanish accent grow thicker than usual. "I don't have to show you any stinkin' badges."

Mace lost it. "Dude, what are you doing here?"

"I stopped by your house. Your parents said this place was my best bet. You've been dropping in the standings, you know," he added, gesturing back toward the sim.

"Don't I know it. But seriously . . . what are you doing here?"

Dex glanced around. He lowered his voice. "Ahmed sent me."

"Ahmed?"

"Dude, this isn't over—not by a long shot."

////// CHAPTER TWENTY-THREE

Mace invited Dex into the house and escorted him over to the kitchen. Mom and Dad sat at the dining table, pecking away at twin laptops. They were both home because Dad had quit his job at the bottling plant. After Mace's payoff, he didn't need to work a second job. Mace was happy about that. At least something good had come out of it all.

Along with a phone for himself, the computers were the first purchases Mace had made when he returned home. The laptops had the latest assistive technologies, and his parents had taken to them like fish to water. They were joining new Deaf community networks. They loved the dictation software, which allowed them to catch up on years of shows and movies that didn't have closed captioning. They were making the most of standard computer tools too. Dad was editing and filing old photos digitally, and Mom had started working again on her novel.

Mace waved as he entered the dining room. They looked up and noticed Dex immediately. "This is my friend from TURBO Summer Academy," Mace hurried to explain. He spoke as well as signing, for Dex's benefit.

They greeted Dex with friendly waves and handshakes. Dex took off his hat. Mom offered a verbal, "He told us he was your friend when he stopped by earlier. Make yourself at home."

"Thank you." Dex smiled.

"Can I borrow one of the computers?" Mace asked, getting right to the point.

"Would you mind waiting a few minutes?" Mom said. "We're on a web conference. But it's wrapping up. Can I get you anything? Sandwiches?"

"No, thanks. We're good on food." Mace grabbed hold of a lapel on Dex's fancy vest and herded him into his bedroom.

"So, what's going on?" Mace asked.

Dex closed the door behind him. Dex began in a low voice, checking over his shoulders. "I was in a sim in Tucson, and—"

"You don't have to whisper," Mace pointed out.

"Oh, right. Sorry." Dex cleared his throat and started over. "I was in Tucson, and this text popped up on the simulator displays: 'Dex, is that you?' And I was like, 'Uh, yeah.' And the texts kept coming. 'This is Ahmed. We need to talk. Can you track down Mace? I can't get ahold of him.'"

"Yeah, I've kind of been avoiding everything since the Philippines," Mace admitted. "I've barely turned on the TV. I've just been sleeping and wandering around. I don't know—today was my first time back to the arcade."

"I know the feeling." Dex sat down on the edge of Mace's messy bed. "But this sounds urgent. Ahmed didn't say more. He gave me a private video call line, told me to call once I found you."

"Did you hear the news about Aya?"

"Yeah, I saw. You guys really made an impression in the Philippines showcase, dude!"

"You know what really happened, right?" Mace asked pointedly.

Dex frowned. "I could guess."

"Henryk shorted my circuits at the last second. Locked up my wheels."

"That's what he did to me!" Dex exclaimed.

"I figured. But here's the crazy thing: I still finished before him. *I* was the pilot of trimorpher *88*. I won that race."

"Wait. Seriously?" Dex shook his head.

"Tempest had a booby trap installed on my ride, too. She told me to use it on him. I refused. So when I won anyway, she just pretended Henryk was in car *88* all along. It's all a lie. It was always a lie. She's looking for a crook, not a TURBO-naut."

They sat in silence until a knock came at the door. Dex opened it and Mom handed over her laptop. "Sure you don't want something to eat?" she asked.

"We're all right. Thank you," Dex said. Mom read his lips.

"Okay. Let me know if you change your mind." She left, closing the door softly.

Mace fired up the laptop and called the number Dex had given him. The video feed connected immediately. A blank screen was replaced with a fish-eye image of Ahmed, framed by a backdrop of server banks and blinking diodes.

"Perfect timing," Ahmed whispered. Mace was rattled by how nervous he looked. "Tempest is topside at the moment. Still, I don't have a lot of time."

Ahmed's words appeared in a text bubble beside the video. Mom hadn't turned off the dictation software, but Mace was so used to this that he was able to ignore it.

"What's going on, Ahmed?"

He took a deep breath, thought for a moment before launching into his answer. "What happened to you in the Philippines—it wasn't right. Tempest is changing everything. She's going to ruin the sport if she has her way. TURBO racing will become a street fight. Oil slicks, smoke screens, grappling hooks, tire shredders, pulse drives, energy shields—she wants to make it all legal."

"Bigger tennis rackets," agreed Mace. "She's been going on about finding the gaps in the rules—and making all the products that'll go in tomorrow's trimorphers."

"And the name Hollande will be everywhere we turn. . . ." Ahmed trailed off for a second. Mace glimpsed in his expression the same frustration he had been feeling. Ahmed continued. "I've been instructed to put all sorts of tricks up Henryk's sleeve. He could accidently kill someone out there.

And if Aya qualifies for the Prix, she'll be one of his targets."

Mace squeezed a fist. "You need to warn her, Ahmed!"

"I have! But she brushes me off. I think Tempest has told her not to worry about Henryk. She believes the lie. She's so focused on proving herself. It's a blind spot for her."

"Then go to the authorities," Dex suggested.

"She'll pay them off, if she hasn't already," Ahmed answered. "I don't know who to trust. And if she finds out I'm going behind her back, she'll just replace me with someone more reliable. We're all better off with me on the inside."

Dex and Mace shared a desperate look. "What do you want us to do?" Mace asked.

Ahmed glanced over his own shoulders nervously, leaned in close. "I want you to race again, Mace."

Mace shook his head. He surprised himself with what he said. "I can't. I'm done."

Ahmed's eyes grew large. "Please, Mace. You're the only 'naut who can beat Henryk in spite of the advantages he'll have. And Tempest has to lose if we're going to save the sport—and protect Aya."

"How? I've got no racer, no team, and not nearly enough money."

"I sent the *Event Horizon* chassis to the Boulder airport. It was stripped of its engine, a few other accessories, but almost everything else is there. If you can get to it . . . If the two of you can figure out how to fix her up . . . I can make sure on my end that you've got a spot waiting for you in the San Fran Pro-Am. Win that, and you automatically—"

"Go on to the Gauntlet Prix—" declared Dex, excitement rising in his voice.

Mace finished the sentence for him, his heart pounding in his chest. "Where we put a stop to Tempest's nonsense."

"And save this sport," added Ahmed. "With Dex's help, you can do it, Mace. I believe in you."

Mace took a deep breath.

Henryk could accidently kill someone out there.

"This is crazy, you know," said Mace.

"It's the only way," Ahmed argued.

Mace looked at Dex. "He's right," Dex agreed. "You're the only one good enough to beat a cheater fair and square."

"All right," he said. "Okay. I'll see what I can do."

"That's all I can ask," said Ahmed. "We have to do this *legit.* And only you can pull that off."

There was a noise off camera. Ahmed's head whipped

around, then darted back. "I have to go. We can't talk again. Too risky. I'm going to scrub this IP. But if you file with the Association by the end of next week, a slot will be waiting. That's my promise. Good luck. And make every morph matter."

The screen went blank, though the dictation software lagged behind, and was still typing out Ahmed's comments. Mace and Dex watched his final words repeat themselves in text form, as if they needed extra help translating what had just gone down.

Mace sat at the edge of his seat, his palms sweaty.

"Ahmed wants us to rebuild *Event Horizon*. In less than two weeks. How is that possible? There's no engine. The landing system . . . Electrical . . . Not to mention jet fuel prices! It's impossible." He clenched his fists. He was . . . so close and so far away.

"There has to be a way to do this," Dex insisted, pacing the room. He absently picked up Mace's scale model of *Iron Dragon* and examined it as he paced.

"I'm not sneaking into the airport again. I barely escaped last time, and my dad still works there. He loves that job. No more breaking the rules—for anything."

A knock came at the door, startling both of them. Dex

reached over and pulled it open. Mace's mom and dad stood in the doorway. They looked uncertain and studied their son closely for a moment. Finally, Dad signed, "M. This wasn't on purpose. But we saw your conversation."

Mom placed the second laptop, open, on the bed. Mace's eyes widened. It was showing an exact duplicate image of the other laptop.

Mace explained to Dex. "They saw the whole thing."

Even as he spoke, his words were dictated to text on both computers, making the situation obvious to both of them.

I'm not sneaking into the airport again.
I barely escaped last time, and my dad
still works there.
He loves that job. No more breaking
the rules—for anything.

Dad continued to sign. "We were on a web conference together. We weren't trying to spy."

Mace watched his parents, realizing that they'd figured out everything.

"I'm so sorry," Mace signed to them. "I don't know how—"

His father signed, "You haven't been the same since you got home. This explains why."

Mace nodded in agreement. "Dad," he started. "Mom." He was scared to say the wrong thing. He didn't want to get into more trouble than he already was. "I've been so selfish and stupid."

"Stupid?" signed Mom. "No. You're just . . . out in front of everybody. It's where you belong."

Dad's eyes were soft. "You hid this because we would have said no. We never understood how good you are at what you do."

Mace's eyes stung but he held the tears back. "TURBO racing isn't what I do," he told them. "It's who I am."

"A big-T TURBOnaut," Dex agreed.

Dad looked at each of the boys in turn, thinking. Dex's comment appeared on the computer screens and seemed to jar something loose in Dad's head. He and Mom shared a long glance. Mom nodded. Dad turned back to his son. He fished a security badge out of his blazer pocket and lassoed it around his neck.

"Time's wasting," he signed. "Let's go to the airport."

///// CHAPTER TWENTY-FOUR

Mace's dad navigated his sedan through the security checkpoint without a hitch. He drove along the restricted-access lot and parked behind the flight-training school, the nearest he could get to the cargo terminal in an unofficial vehicle.

The boys peeked out from under a tarp in the back of the car. Dad signed, "Let me have a look. I'll see if I can locate this thing. Is it boxed?"

"I have no idea," Mace responded.

The door banged shut. The minutes dragged on. And on. Mace started to worry that his dad had found trouble instead of *Event Horizon*. How much had Dad risked to come here and snoop around? What was his cover story? But Mace's worries were unfounded. Dad finally returned, filled with childish excitement, and opened the rear passenger door so quickly that Mace spilled onto the concrete before he could brace himself.

"Stay down," Dad ordered. "Wait till the security camera turns."

A few seconds later, he hurried Mace and Dex along the flight school wall and around the corner. The airport was in operation but not very busy. A few employees shuffled to and fro, and a couple trucks and specialized vehicles carried out their business. Dad handed each of the boys an employee ball cap and giant orange earmuffs. "Wear these. Act like you belong here. Stand straight. No one will bother with you unless they see you up close."

Mace relayed the instructions to Dex, and they both nodded.

"In here." Dad beckoned to them.

They entered the cargo facility through a side door. Dad led them through a series of carpeted hallways and stopped at a metal door with a window. Beyond was a warehouse space lit only by natural sunlight coming in through small, high windows. "Look in there. There're several vehicle-sized crates on pallets. Could one of them be it?"

Dex poked into the storage area and glanced around. He gave the "all clear." The three of them fanned out to inspect the five crates.

None of the wooden containers were marked with descriptions that meant anything. Giant barcodes, stenciled letters that said *This Side Up*, and that was it. They were all nailed shut, except for one, which had a lid with hinges and was secured with combination padlocks.

"That's the one," Mace said.

"How can you tell?" asked Dex.

"Because Ahmed knows I'm good with combo locks."

Mace gripped the first lock gently and turned the dial clockwise and counterclockwise. *Click. Tap. Clack.* Yank.

It opened, no problem.

"I don't remember Ahmed giving you codes," said Dex.

"He didn't. There's no need," Mace told him. He winked, opened the next lock without ever looking at it, having fun.

It took all three of them to open the lid. A quick glance inside revealed that Mace was right.

"There she is," Mace whistled. The black trimorpher was tucked into submersible form, its most compact configuration. The fold-up job was far from seamless, though. The damage to the hull prevented a tight fit. The glass canopy was new. Totally intact. A gift from Ahmed, Mace figured. But the rest of it looked more banged up than he had remembered. He wondered if they'd be able to fix it.

They quietly dropped the lid back into place. Mace looped the locks through their latches but didn't close them. "How are we going to get this out of here?" he whispered and signed.

"I have an idea," signed Dad. "Wait here."

A few minutes later, he was backing a scuffed, unlabeled delivery truck into the storage bay. He cut the engine, jumped down, and rolled up the back door. "We're inside a restricted area," he explained. "Keys to these things are always on the dash. I'll be right back with the forklift," he said. "Climb inside the truck to stay out of sight."

The boys obeyed. Mace felt a bit useless as they watched Dad trot off and return a minute later, behind the wheel of a large forklift. Just as he secured the prongs through the pallet spacers, a guy in a hard hat strolled into view and raised his hand.

Mace and Dex shrank back into the delivery truck's interior. Mace could hear his heartbeat in his ears.

Dad shut off the engine and climbed down. The employee asked him what he was doing. Dad silently signed back to him. They went back and forth, not understanding each other, for a good twenty seconds, before the guy embraced the fact that he was trying to talk to someone who couldn't hear. He scratched under his hard hat.

Dad showed him his security clearance. He escorted the guy over to the crate and demonstrated how the combination locks were all open. He signed at the guy, "It's scrap metal. Just taking it to the junk heap." The man in the hard hat didn't understand a word. He shoved a clipboard at Dad, gestured for Dad to write it down. Dad retold his story on paper.

The hardhat man stared at the dangling locks.

"Okay, okay." He waved Dad off. "Go on. Sorry to bother."

Dad patted him on the back and promptly jumped up behind the wheel of the forklift. A moment later, the boys were squeezing out of the way as the crate was guided into the back of the truck.

"No one's going to miss this shipment, right?" his father asked.

Mace shrugged. "Ahmed's not going to report it missing."

Dad closed the truck door, moving quickly. "Stay back here. Once we get to the house we'll push the crate out on the curb. If I get the truck back here before the next cargo plane needs unloading at two, no one will be the wiser."

Twenty minutes later, Mom was helping the three of them shove the wooden crate out of the delivery truck. Trimophers were designed to be relatively light. Even so, *Event Horizon*, empty of fuel and missing its engine, was lighter than Mace expected. The wood slid nicely along the aluminum siding of the truck interior. Gravity did the rest.

The box slammed down onto the street. Dex winced, but Mace laughed. "It's not like it's in mint condition."

Dad peeled away in the delivery truck, racing the clock.

Mom stood with her arms crossed, inspecting the giant crate that had been dumped half on, half off the sidewalk in front of their house. Neighbors were peering out their barred windows. A small kid on a bike rode by, staring, and almost slammed into a mailbox. Mom unfolded her arms to say, "Mace, we can't leave this here. You can't keep it at the house. What are you going to do with it?"

Mace had been wondering the same thing. It was impractical and insecure to think of rebuilding a trimorpher streetside. If the news caught wind of what they were up to, if Tempest heard about it . . .

But then he had an idea.

"Mom, can you text your boss for me?"

"I suppose. What for?"

"Ask him where he keeps *Brown Trout*."

She reached into her pocket but stopped, giving him a quizzical look.

"Trust me, just ask him."

CHAPTER TWENTY-FIVE //////

Robert Gerber's head emerged from behind the crumpled hood of *Event Horizon*. "Oh, man," he said. "Someone pinch me."

The workbench-lined room wasn't large by any means, but it was spacious enough to fit the damaged chassis and allow a few people enough room to maneuver. "This thing's a beaut. I can't even begin to process all this, Mace."

They were inside the Gerbers' old barn, which had been converted into a stand-alone garage behind their large home. The property had once been a working farm. It was perfect for Mace. He and Dex would have tons of privacy, a full suite of tools, and the enthusiasm of a man who built trimorphers in his spare time. *Brown Trout*, carefully covered in a fine tarpaulin cloth, had been shoved into a side nook of the former barn to give *Event Horizon* center stage.

Mace circled around to Mr. Gerber, brushing his fingertips along the hull. "So, is it doable?" he asked.

Mr. Gerber stroked his mustache, making calculations. "We're short a few tools. I can fix the landing gear, get everything wired up right. But the frame is bent. I don't have what it takes to straighten her, or to smooth out the hull. Normally I'd send away for new panels, have them welded in town, but you don't have time for that."

"I'm working on a solution for the structural damage," Mace said. "But you're okay with helping us out, giving the other repairs a shot?"

Mr. Gerber laughed. "I already had my secretary clear my calendar straight through the Pro-Am. Not going to miss this for the world. I still can't get over it, Mace. I can't believe that was you behind the wheel, blowing past me over the seas with that barrel roll! I laughed so hard when that happened. I knew I was witnessing real talent."

Carson, who had been pacing in the shadows, had finally

had enough and ducked out the back door of the workshop, letting it slam shut behind him. Mace winced. Taking all this in must've been tough for the Gerb.

"Let's get to work." Dex hopped off the edge of a nearby counter.

"We should start with a general inventory of what we'll need," Mr. Gerber agreed. "Tools and parts. I'll make sure my computer diagnostics software is compatible with your interface. A lot of this craft's innards look proprietary, but we'll figure it out. I'm really curious: what did you have in mind for straightening the hull out?"

At that moment, the answer arrived. Mom and Dad walked through the side door, escorting a guest. "Funny you should ask. Mr. Gerber, meet Mr. Hernandez, my metal-shop teacher."

Mr. Hernandez shook Robert's hand, then turned to Mace. "What is this? What's going on here?"

Mace had tried to explain everything over the phone. His teacher knew the general basics, probably just wanted a bit of reassurance. Mace pointed to *Event Horizon*. "Can you unbend that for us?"

The metal-shop teacher's eyes lit up. He whistled, approaching the craft with reverence. "Mace," he said incredulously. That was the only word he said. He lost himself for a few minutes inspecting the vehicle and its movable parts.

Until finally: "I can make this work." Mr. Hernandez smiled. "Some of these alloys don't bend back so easily. But we can cut out the buckled bits. I can fashion replacements at the school shop, then bring them over and weld them in."

"That's great!" exclaimed Dex. "We're in business!"

"Funny thing, though,"—Mr. Hernandez eyed Mace suspiciously—"my canister of welding gas went missing at the end of the school year."

Mace released a guilty, nervous chuckle. "Um. Tell you what. I'll take care of that for you. I'll get a, um, replacement canister out to you right away."

"How generous of you." Mr. Hernandez winked at him.

Dad tapped Mace. "Son. You were in that thing when it got all bent out of shape?"

Uh-oh. His parents looked worried. They looked like they were having second thoughts about all of this. Mace thought through his next words carefully. "I was," he admitted, signing. "I never felt a thing. I was perfectly safe. And I landed so hard on purpose. It was the only way I could win."

"But how did you not feel anything?" Mom asked.

"Come here," invited Mace. "Take a seat." He popped open the canopy.

Carson entered the garage, one hand in a hoodie pocket, the other holding a can of orange soda. The hoodie was one of his daily rotating Gauntlet League jerseys: the slate gray and crimson of *Guillotine*, the chopper-morpher piloted by the French phenom Leon "Napoleon" Dubois. Twenty-four years old. Weak on his left side. Especially during morphs. Mace laughed at himself. Tempest had drilled him so hard with stats that the details still came to him in an effortless wave.

Carson's expression was stiff and guarded, but he joined the circle of people and watched as Mace's mom nervously climbed into the submersible's cockpit.

"What are you planning, Mace?" she said aloud, signing for Dad's benefit. She laughed nervously. "I'm not sure about this."

"You're fine. Just sit down all the way. I'm going to show you something," Mace signed while he spoke. He glanced at Carson, whose expression was no longer guarded, but confused and uncertain.

Dad signed, "Take her for a spin!"

"Don't you dare turn this thing on while I'm in it." Mom was adamant.

"Ready?" asked Mace. "Here we go." He pushed a button on a light display. The smart cushioning took over. Mom sank into the bucket seat with a surprised yelp, and then yelped again when the seat hardened around her, encasing her in position.

"This stuff absorbs all the blows," Mace explained. "And plus, if the situation gets really bad, and I can't eject, there's emergency foam that'll expand and fill the cockpit instantaneously."

"Okay, I get it." Mom surrendered. "Just let me out!"

Carson was watching Mace. Mace watched him right back. While the others were absorbed in discussing the trimorpher's various features, Carson came up to him.

"Hey, I, uh, I want to tell you something." The Gerb squirmed for some reason.

"Uh, what's that?" Mace played along, a little nervous. He'd never seen Carson appear so . . . genuine.

"You never told me your parents were deaf."

"You seriously had no idea?" Mace shook his head and laughed.

"I—I'm sorry," stammered Carson. "About . . . making fun of that . . . around you, last year. I get now why you slugged me."

Mace stared, frozen, at the strange alien talking to him. "Oh," he said. "Well, thank you. Apology accepted. And I'm . . . I'm sorry, too."

Carson raised an eyebrow. "So, um. Can I help?"

Mace smiled. "Yeah, sure! Of course! Come on. Dive right in." They joined the rest of the team, deep in a conversation about the game plan.

"That's all well and good," Mr. Hernandez was pointing out. "But we're missing an engine! Other replacement parts, too. That's the final piece of the puzzle. I mean, I'm happy to chip in with time and tools, but, uh, I'm a public-school teacher. Who's gonna pay for everything we need?"

Dad tapped on Mace's shoulder. "I can raid the airport boneyard," he offered. "Tell me what you need, and I'll see what I can find."

"That's a great idea," Mace signed. "Thank you."

"And, M.," Mom added. "That money you got paid? Dad and I discussed this." They shared a tacit nod. "That money is yours. Use it if you need to."

"But, Dad, you just quit your job."

"I can go back to the bottling plant. That's just a job. This is your dream. Whatever it takes. Win that Glove. Then we'll all retire."

"I can't take it anymore!" Mr. Gerber had been pacing the room, stroking his mustache, when he stopped and shouted. All eyes were on him. "Sometimes in life you just gotta go all in. This is our moment. Let's show them what we're made of!"

"Dad," Carson said, embarrassed. "Spit it out. What are you talking about?"

Robert strode over to *Brown Trout.* He whipped the tarpaulin off.

That yellow! So. Yellow. Someone gasped. Mace held back a laugh.

"Uh, Dad?" Carson asked. "Tell me you're not entering the Pro-Am."

"No!" Mr. Gerber waved the idea away. "You think I'm crazy?"

The Gerb was more than happy to reply. "We've already established this: yes."

"No," Mr. Gerber smiled. He turned to Mace. "You need an engine? I've got an engine. It's all yours. To borrow, I mean."

He reached a hand into *Brown Trout's* cockpit and popped

open the rear side panels, revealing an elegant, spotless, silver-plated Rolls-Royce Pegasus X-90. Class D.

The most powerful rocket engine ever approved for non-military use. Now at Mace's disposal.

////// CHAPTER TWENTY-SIX

Dex escorted Mace into the garage, his hands cupped over Mace's eyes. "You ready?"

Mace took a deep breath. Ready? He'd waited his entire life for this moment. The past week had been ten times more exhausting than Tempest's "academy." Very little sleep. Very little food. The days and nights had blended together, unnoticed. But the combined effort of his friends had paid off. *Event Horizon* was restored.

At least in theory.

When he'd last seen it, the new-and-improved *Event*

Horizon had reminded Mace of his Frankenstein bike. A jumble of mismatched parts and shades of gray, blotched with chips of leftover black paint and patches of sanded-down fiberglass. Mr. Gerber had plugged the central processor into his diagnostic mainframe to let a series of comprehensive tests run their course for twenty-four hours.

Now Mace was back, ready to review the results of the tests, which would tell him whether the vehicle was safe enough to take out for a test drive.

"Three, two, one," said Dex, and he uncovered Mace's eyes.

"Surprise!" a room full of people shouted.

Mace couldn't take it all in at once. He saw the people first. His team. Mr. Gerber and Carson. Mr. Hernandez. Mace's parents. Dex. They had all worked so hard for this, given so much of themselves to the effort. Mace hadn't expected everyone to be here tonight. His heart swelled.

He saw the banner next, tied off at either end and draped from the ceiling. Dark orange words on a midnight-blue background, with cream and silver highlighting.

Go, Renegade!

Tempest's own words echoed in his inner ear: *I want you to come at this whole sport sideways. The cops, over Denver.*

Remember? They called you a . . .

"Renegade," he said.

"Do you like it?" asked Dex hopefully. "Your racing name."

You have to earn it.

"Renegade. It's perfect." Mace beamed.

And then he saw the roadster—polished and gleaming, painted in just-before-dawn blue, with a burnt-orange, fading glow silhouetting a Rocky Mountain horizon all along the mid hull. The differences went beyond the paint job. This trimorpher had new fins and contours and other details trimmed in silver and cream.

"She's gorgeous," he finally managed. "I can't wait to get behind the wheel."

"Go ahead," Mr. Gerber invited. He opened the canopy. "Hop in."

"Wait," said Mace. "I thought we needed to review the diagnostics."

Mr. Hernandez smiled. "Those tests only took eight hours. We've been here all day, painting and fine-tuning. We wanted to surprise you. She's ready."

"Really?" Mace asked. His feet carried him, one step at a time, forward.

Mace reached out to the blue-and-orange trimorpher and placed his hands on her.

Somewhere deep inside, she purred. *Yes.* This was her. Only better.

"Hey, gal," he said. The others backed away to give him room. He walked all the way around her.

He didn't need eight hours of diagnostics to confirm that she was shipshape.

"Let's take her for a spin," he told everyone.

"Don't forget this," Carson said. He thrust something out at Mace.

A polished, dark-blue helmet and a flight suit with burnt orange trim.

Mace took the offering, incredulous. It was exactly like the one he'd worn during training. "Where'd you get this?" he asked.

Dex fessed up. "It's mine. But we know they're all the same size. I, um, kept it when I left. And now it's yours."

"I put my star tailor in charge of the redesign," Mr. Gerber added. "The original flexibility of the fabric should be intact."

"Thank you. Why don't you wear it, Dex?" Mace asked.

"You can fly 'er just as well as—"

"Nope, nope, nope." Dex shook his head. "I'm not as fast as you. I always knew that. Besides, this isn't just a copy of *Event Horizon*. This is *Event Horizon*. No way I could ride this bull the way you can."

Mace gave Dex a fist bump. He offered one to Carson as well.

"Dex and I will be your comm," Carson told him. "No one else knows the ropes the way we do. We'll have your back every second of every race."

Mace nodded, too choked up to try to speak. They all watched as he slipped on his flight suit and fastened his helmet.

He crawled inside the cockpit.

"All right, Renegade," Dex said. "She needs a name, too."

"She's always been *Event Horizon* to me." Mace shrugged. "Let me get a feel for her. I'm sure the right name will come."

"Great," Dex agreed. "There are a few mods you'll want to get a handle on. They're mostly for looks but might tighten the handling. We didn't want her to be recognizable as *Event Horizon*. Better have a name picked out by the time you get back."

Mace sank into the smart cushioning and closed the canopy.

The garage door opened. Mace fired the beast up, and immediately felt the familiarity of an old friend's embrace. "It's you, all right," he said. "Let's see what you got."

He rolled over the gravel driveway and gunned it down the street.

From the inside, the craft was the same. Mace's hands blindly sought out dozens of levers and switches and light displays with innate precision. The craft operated as she had before. She was every bit as powerful, still a generation ahead of her time. The machinery beneath the hood and beneath Mace's seat breathed and hummed the same as ever. But Mace detected a new edge.

The Pegasus X-90 was hungry to show off what it could do.

He took a tight curve on the dark road and found he could give it a little more fuel than before. The vehicle hugged the curve like Velcro. No fishtailing. Over the course of hundreds of ground laps, that could mean *minutes* shaved off his time.

Maybe that was her name—Razor? Shaver? Blade?

No, no, no. All terrible.

How was he supposed to name her? It was too big of a decision.

We're in this together. The name has something to do with both of us.

Kindred Spirit? No. Way too sentimental.

Mace zoomed past a sign for a trailhead leading to a prairie with rolling hills. On a whim, he morphed to air and doubled back to tackle the grassland using a trail of his own.

Dark blue and burnt orange. Day glow against the stratosphere. *Skywalker?*

Nope. Taken.

The moonlit trail switchbacked along the silvery hills. It came to him, courtesy of his mom.

You're just . . . out in front of everybody. It's where you belong.

He and the craft, they both carved their own path. They were each a . . .

"Pathfinder."

No. That wasn't quite right, either. Mace wasn't finding something that was already there. He was making this up from scratch.

What was it Tempest had said to him, early on? *If no*

one's blazing trails, Mace, the world has nowhere to go.

"Trailblazer."

Mace said the word several times aloud. *Yes,* he thought. *That's it.*

"Trailblazer," he said. "Let's go blaze a trail."

He leaned into the throttle and gunned it for the snow-capped Rockies on the starry horizon.

////// CHAPTER TWENTY-SEVEN

Inside Team *Trailblazer*'s hospitality tent, Dex secured the straps on Mace's midnight-blue helmet. He stood back to examine his friend. "Renegade. Look at you."

Mace was unable to summon his voice. Dex's jumpsuit fit him perfectly. The silky, honeycomb texture wicked away his sweat and kept him cool. He felt taller in the boots and was grateful for that, too.

Beyond the flapping white canvas walls, the Bay Area crowds roared. What Mace knew about San Francisco, he'd learned from his afternoon tour of the course yesterday.

The streets ran straight up and down super-steep hills. The Golden Gate Bridge, always draped in fog, was breathtaking. Alcatraz, the prison island of old, sat right in the bay for all to see, its stone facades rising up out of rock of the same color. Skybox blimps were tethered in place by red cables that mimicked the suspension cables on the Golden Gate Bridge. *Cool touch,* Mace had thought.

The crowd roared again, bringing him back to now. Introductions of each TURBOnaut were underway. "Hey, is that Talon?" Carson nudged Mace to ask.

Mace peeked out of his tent and laughed. "Yeah, it is." Talon! Only a few feet away. He stood relaxed next to his racer. One of the biggest stars of them all, he looked totally at ease in his shiny red-and-black racing suit. Blue-tinted aviator glasses contrasted strikingly with his spiky blond hair.

"Let's go say hi," Carson said. "There's time. C'mon . . ."

Mace wanted to, but something held him back. "I better keep a low profile." But he saw the excitement in Carson's eyes. He couldn't help cracking a grin. "You go."

"You sure?"

"Get him to sign something for me too," Mace suggested. "See you in the pit."

Carson was embarrassed about it for a beat, but then he ran off toward the famous TURBOnaut.

A moment later, Mace heard a familiar name from the announcer. "And now please give a warm welcome to Katana, the rising-star pilot of *Lotus*."

"Katana," Mace said to Dex. "*Lotus*. Tempest let her choose those names. I wonder why she didn't let Henryk choose *Mjölnir*."

"Don't worry about her," Dex told him. "Worry about the wind around Sears Point. Not so much over the bay. Be cautious with your launch to air. Pay attention to the wind socks. A third-place finish or better, and you advance to the Prix."

"Third place or better," repeated Mace.

A horn honked in front of the luffing tent door. The truck that would transport Mace to the start line had arrived. Mace took a deep breath. This was it. The time had come for him to turn and stand and face the world alone.

"Go show them what you're made of," said Dex. "Make every morph matter."

"Thank you for everything," Mace told him. "You're a true friend."

"We're family, bro."

Mace exited the tent and climbed into the back of the truck. The vehicle was an advertisement for a local car dealership—all part of the theatrics of the starting line. He and the driver shot each other mock salutes, and they paraded forward onto the track.

"And without further ado, we're pleased to announce a new personality to the sport, making their debut appearance right here in San Francisco. Ladies and gentlemen, fans of all ages, please give a big welcome to Renegade, piloting *Trailblazer.*"

Mace wore foam earpieces. Additionally, the padding built into the helmet deafened him, but he could still hear the stadium crowds. They answered the announcer with equal parts cheering, hissing, booing, and polite applause.

The Pro-Am would begin and end on the two-mile ground track of the Sonoma Raceway. The grandstands and terraces hosted over sixty thousand spectators, and the hospitality tents, stages, and overhead skyboxes were full of additional fans, every one of them staring at Mace Blazer as he approached the lineup of other TURBOnauts.

What am I doing out here? There's been a terrible mistake.

The other 'nauts each stood beside their roadsters.

Except for Katana, their helmets all rested in their arms, their faces plain to see. They watched Mace approach, his face covered. The compulsion to take off his own helmet was nearly overwhelming.

Mace jumped down off the truck. He studied the other TURBOnauts as he strode over to *Trailblazer*, recognizing all of them. Most were in their early twenties. Talon was at the head of the pack. His burnt-red helmet gleamed under his arm. Near him was Taz Nazaryan, who drove *Pitchfork*, a maroon-and-gold-striped roadster. Shaped more like a stock car than most other trimorphers, it would turn into a respectable airplane and skimmer—but it ruled the ground track, gripping the asphalt like no other.

"With fifty ground laps to start the race, Taz will lap you by the time you launch to air," Carson had warned him. "Don't sweat it. Know it's inevitable, but stay as close as you can and overtake him in the air as soon as possible."

On and on down the line, Mace identified the competition, recalling important notes. *Apocalypse*'s Randall Horseman: older, but a former Glove winner. He always wore his Golden Gauntlet while racing. Akshara Brahma and *Untouchable*. They'd been on a tear all year. Ariel Pterin was inspecting *Pterodactyl*. Bethany Ironsides was next to *Blacksmith*. All of them had already qualified for the Prix.

Carpe Diem. Yolo "YOLO" Volkov was Europe's hottest commodity behind *Guillotine*'s Leon "Napoleon" Dubois. *Castle. Monsoon. Five Alarm. Ursa Major.* Forty competitors, all told. About a quarter of them amateurs. Mace glazed over those, uninterested, unconcerned, until he came to the next-to-last roadster in line.

The green-and-lavender *Lotus.* Standing poised beside her: Katana.

Aya, dressed in a new metallic-green flight suit, was the only other 'naut already wearing her helmet. Mace caught her watching him through her polished, eggplant-colored visor. "Katana," he said. He nodded in her direction. She studied him closely.

She must suspect that Mace was Renegade. Tempest would be suspicious, too. Both Renegade and *Trailblazer* would raise alarm bells for her. But it was too late. Mace was on the track. There was nothing Tempest could do to stop him now.

Robert Gerber, *Trailblazer*'s crew chief, greeted Mace on the tarmac. They circled the craft, feeling every inch of it for imperfections. The ground was sticky, covered with Coca-Cola—on purpose—to give the racing wheels better traction coming off the start line.

"You notice anything off about the unified fuel control?" asked Mace.

Mr. Gerber gave the hood a pat. "It's temperature sensitive, but should adjust to the Northern California weather long before you go airborne."

Mace cocked his head questioningly.

Mr. Gerber gave his mustache a stroke. "Nothing gets by you. Your throttle's locked at ninety-percent capacity, Mace. I dialed it back so you don't kill yourself out there. Trust me, even at ninety percent, *Trailblazer*'s still more powerful than almost anything else. Keep your training wheels on until I'm convinced you can handle the extra g's."

"Okay." Mace frowned. "I have manual override for that, yeah?"

Mr. Gerber gave him a long, hard look. "Don't touch it unless I give the go-ahead. Which I won't. Winning is great—but coming home alive and in one piece is WAY more important."

Carson came back in time to help Mace into his seat and

to help him perform the safety checks and last-minute diagnostic run-throughs.

Carson punched his shoulder. “You got this, Renegade.”

Mace grinned. “Let’s hope there’s no chain-link fences out there.”

“Nothing’ll stop you this time.” Carson winked.

Mace gave him a gloved thumbs-up, glad his face was hidden behind a visor. “I’m choking up in here. Honestly, there might be tears,” he replied, trying to sound like he was joking.

Carson laughed and shut the top glass canopy. He and the rest of the crew backed away. The cheers of the crowd became a roar like nothing Mace had ever heard. It sifted through the glass, its very own kind of silence.

“Okay,” he told himself. “Now you can look.”

He glanced to his right. Directly across from him, in the first row, sat his parents.

They were holding hands. They saw him looking and waved.

The high sun was at just the right angle to illuminate the cockpit interiors without creating too much glare on the glass canopies. This was no accident, of course. Starting-line ticketholders expected their money's worth of exclusive views. He waved back.

The distance and barriers and noise between them were irrelevant. His dad signed. "Get out there. Show the world who you are."

"I will," he promised.

"Nervous?" Mom asked.

Mace laughed. He pinched his fingers together, showed them. "Just a little bit."

"Don't be," she answered. "Just be yourself. Big-T TURBO racer! But promise me: no speeding," she added.

Mace leaned back and laughed.

The announcer's bold voice came through the cockpit's closed-circuit radio loud and clear. "Ladies and gentlemen, start your engines!"

The novice pilot just ahead of him—England's Fenny Adder—revved the engine of *Cauldron*. Aya answered beside him, and the familiar rattle of *Lotus* came alive. "This is awe-some!" Mace screamed.

Dex's voice in his earpiece came to life, barely audible over the roar of the start line. "Um? What are you waiting for?"

Laughing at himself, he realized he'd forgotten to turn on *Trailblazer.* He punched the ignition, and his faithful steed awoke beneath him. A wild grin stole over his face. This race was different. He was here on his own terms, and this was the first race of his life that really mattered.

Let her breathe. Listen to her. She'll do the heavy lifting. He could tell: *Trailblazer* was hungry for an honest win. Then he relaxed, a new realization overcoming him like a warm embrace:

So was he.

///// CHAPTER TWENTY-EIGHT

Mace was tense in his seat, his palms sweaty.

The pace car led the way, and the grid of roadster-phase trimorphers gathered speed as they entered the first bend of the Sonoma Raceway. The roadsters jostled to the right and left, priming the tires by heating them and scuffing them of factory oils. Mace swerved, too, visualizing a path through the cars ahead, all while accelerating. The tires developed a sticky grip on the road; his handling was tight, fluid. More speed. Everything beyond the other racers became a blur. There was only the swarm of huddled vehicles, the rhythm of the changing slope as straightaways became tight curves.

He came around the final bend and caught a glimpse of the grandstands. A green flag danced and waved in the distance. Talon, Taz, Yolo, Akshara, and the other leaders were already across the start line at full speed, breaking from the pack, banking into the first curve of the first official lap. The race had begun. The squadron of roadsters directly in front of Mace lurched forward, no distant pace car holding them back.

Mace gunned it, eager to stay on them.

His heart beat wildly.

"Game on!" Dex gleefully shouted in his ears. "Get up in there. Take Aya on the left. You know she hates that. Rattle her early."

The curve eased up, giving him an opening. He found *Trailblazer*'s rhythm; it pulsed up through the steering column into his gloved palms, calming him down. He rocketed past two novices, leaving them tied for last place, and entered the next turn tightly holding to the inside lane, gaining ground and passing Aya.

Mace had no doubt she'd make him answer for that before too long.

"Fantastic. Now you're racing. Keep it up. I want you halfway through the standings by the time you leave the raceway."

Forty competitors. I need to be in twentieth place by the fiftieth lap. That meant leaving someone in his dust about every other lap. *That's doable,* he thought. His muscles grew steady as he passed another two stragglers. By lap ten, he was already in thirtieth place, and starting to feel good about his chances.

He accelerated and inched up on the other roadsters. "Any chance I can just . . . morph to air for a split second, kinda jump the other racers?"

"We're following the rules, right?" Dex asked. Mace could hear the wink in his voice.

"Okay."

"Well, then, you know the drill: you need at least two wheels on the ground during any ground run."

"Only two? Why only two now?"

"New rule. Because some of the skimmers, when they're roadsters, they tend to pop wheelies during aggressive acceleration."

Reports came in that Taz was in the lead. He, Akshara,

and Talon were already exiting the stadium. Mace's eyes widened. How would he ever catch them?

But then he remembered: this race was a long haul. Ten repetitions to boot. They hadn't gone airborne yet. Plenty of time to catch up.

Aya passed him. He passed her. She zoomed by him again, this time leaving him struggling for breath. Tempest had really worked with her ground racing. He let her go.

Focus on the rest of the amateurs. Worry about Aya at the finish line.

Mace completed the fifty ground laps at the Sonoma Raceway. He followed the nearest racers onto the highway to San Pablo Bay, which connected to San Francisco Bay.

He registered a TV tower filled with cameras, and then it was gone in a blur. Up ahead, *Vulcan* was in his sights. He grinned, positioned himself in Caldera Kahale's blind spot, and took her on the left, half on and half off the road's shoulder. He blazed past her, watching as she braked—she actually braked!—startled by the cloud of dust he'd kicked up as he blew by.

"You're killing it, Mace!" Carson sounded positively gleeful. "Don't let up."

San Pablo Bay glistened in his crosshairs. He watched several roadsters take the ramp up ahead at full throttle, transform in midair, and then dive below his line of sight.

The ramp was coming too quickly. He tapped the brakes.

"Don't slow down! This is your first morph," Dex barked. "Everyone's watching! You want every crew out here reporting that you're an easy target during morphs?"

"Good point." The ramp was beneath him. Through sheer instinct and training, his hand found the morph. He toggled it.

He pierced the surface of the bay. His smart cushioning grabbed him and held him back. His Pegasus engine dialed wide, transforming into a turbine. It extended and churned. Mace let out a pent-up cry. No cracks in the canopy. He'd survived. All in all, not a bad morph.

A skimmer shot overhead, zooming past him, but then flipped like a playing card on the rough surface. *Disqualified,* Mace thought smugly. *During the first rep! I'm guaranteed not to come in last place now.*

"Hey, Mace," Mr. Gerber chimed in. "Don't forget to calibrate your dorsal flaps. You're cutting through the current at a twenty-degree angle. Compensate manually. That should give you your speed back."

"Thanks," he said, leaning forward to execute a series of commands on the control panels. He felt a lurch of speed and overtook the next submersible.

He passed a series of underwater camera drones. A giant ring materialized through the murky haze. He shot through the center of it, no sweat. The wind had churned up a ton of sediment in the bay. Mace relaxed his eyes and sensed each ring before it became visible in the haze. He corrected early and often, flying through hoop after hoop while gaining speed.

He jostled past four TURBOnauts on the route to Angel Island and knocked one of them off course. *Castle* veered wide in Mace's wake, missing a hoop, which would cost her a five-second penalty.

Dex encouraged him. "You embarrassed a veteran. Great work."

Mace glanced up, detecting a pair of approaching skimmers. The colors were muted, but he caught sight of the numbers on their bellies easily enough. 74 and 22. *Chariot* and *Excalibur.* They were dueling it out up there, neck and neck, physically nudging each other as they navigated the buoys they had to nail to get time credit. Mace was impressed. Tangling at those speeds was extremely dangerous on the water's surface. *I wouldn't be surprised if one of them—yup.*

The belly of *Excalibur* lifted out of sight, skipped, lifted again, and then rolled. A crash.

"Pendragon's out!" Carson reported. "A huge break for us! Arthur MacLeod won't advance to the Prix, now."

"What about *Chariot*?" Mace asked.

"Apollo Milan will pass over you for sure. Take him back later."

"*Sonar*'s catching up, too," Dex advised. "But this is her strongest terrain. You'll beat them both back the second you're in the air."

"Got it." Mace could feel a submersible on his tail. *Sonar*'s Melanie O'Campo made her move, cutting beneath Mace with a burst of speed. She bulleted forward and disappeared in the haze ahead. A torpedo. But she'd be low-hanging fruit on the other terrains.

The course was changing. The buoys anchored beneath the surface, marking the underwater track boundaries, narrowed and trended shallower. The bellies of coast-guard ships flanked the track. Mace licked his lips. The morph to air was coming up.

"Time to prep for launch. Your approach isn't crowded, which'll give you a—"

"Quiet. I got this." Mace knew what to do. He could execute a morph to air in his sleep. But he wanted this to go perfectly. This was his greeting to the world.

He tilted upward to the angle of ascent. He could feel in the bones of his ears that his inclination was spot on, that his speed was exact.

The nose of the submersible crossed the water's surface. He morphed at the right moment, that space of time between heartbeats, when the breathing of *Trailblazer* came to rest, and salt water ran in rivulets off the fins. The craft sprouted wings, hovering above the water on forward momentum alone. The water droplets floated as suspended spheres. The turbine dialed shut. The jet engine opened and ignited.

He bounded upward into the blue sky over San Francisco, eyes everywhere. He spotted the leaders, flashes of unmistakable color over the city. *Iron Dragon*, *Pitchfork*,

Radioactive, Pterodactyl, and *Blacksmith* were holding a horizontal V formation over downtown. A second pack of air-craft in a second V pattern were dipping beneath the Golden Gate Bridge. “How are they so far ahead?” he said. “More than half an air-lap away!”

“You’ve got your work cut out,” Dex’s voice agreed in his ear. “Now shut your jaw and open your thrusters.”

CHAPTER TWENTY-NINE //////

"Everything gets faster now," Mr. Gerber pointed out. "You have to gun it. But this track is tight. Don't lose control. You can't afford to miss any checkpoints."

Each rep of the Pro-Am course included ten air-laps.

"What place are the dicer pilots in?"

Lotus, *Guillotine*, *Carpe Diem*, and three other choppers were duking it out on a route well within the outer flight path. They were putting on an acrobatic show for the Bay Area audiences, diving and rising, zigging and zagging, through drone-supported checkpoints that resembled a motocross track hovering over Alcatraz and the Presidio.

"Don't worry about them," said Dex. "The courses connect back up. Just get up into that first pack of aircraft."

Mace throttled up. The rocket engine purred. *Trailblazer* responded to his every whim; even with his engine trimmed to ninety percent power, there was nothing the competition could do to beat back his trimorpher.

They had built a one-of-a-kind workhorse. Within seconds of soaring upward, he had left *Sonar* behind. *Stay in control . . .* Mace veered to the right, punching through the middle of the first checkpoint, no problem. He gained speed, his sights set on his next victim: *Chariot*. Apollo Milan's skimmer phase boasted one of the more impressive morphs to air, with its underbelly rising and separating to form wings. Mace slipped ahead of *Chariot* and zipped past the first of the Bay's tethered blimp skyboxes. Spectators cheered wildly as he rocketed past.

Mace overtook another aircraft, and then another. As he banked around the headlands, he joined the tail of a pack of four fliers. Using the group's wake, he broke formation and flung himself forward with a burst of saved-up thrust. He ducked under the Golden Gate Bridge and unleashed the afterburner. He soared over San Francisco, passing above Aya and a swarm of dicers below, accelerating past skyscrapers topped with fans.

The next pack of aircraft hit the following checkpoint in a defensive, spaced-out diamond formation. They were intentionally denying him a wake to coast within. Mace couldn't break through. "They've wised up." Mace gritted his teeth. No matter. *If I can't go through them, I'll go around.* The nearest checkpoint was in his rearview. The course opened up. Mace veered wide.

Really wide.

"What are you up to, Mace?" asked Dex. "Wide arcs mean longer distances."

"Let's do geometry lessons later," he answered. Mace shot in front of the blockade with a sharp swoop, blasting through the next checkpoint before they could nudge him out. He felt the smart cushioning strain under the additional g's, but the tension released as he gained on the next straightaway.

Air-lap after air-lap, Mace crept up on the leaders. His open path felt more like a time trial. This was how he'd trained, learning to race the clock and push his limits. He felt comfortable and it showed. "Faster," he kept telling himself. "Go faster."

"Careful, Mace," Mr. Gerber sang in his ears. "You're at the edge of physics here. The g-forces will squish your brain if you try to cut these turns with too much thrust."

The edge of physics, Mace thought. *Sounds awesome.*

Air-lap ten. *Pitchfork*, *Iron Dragon*, and *Untouchable* were in his sights. "I've got a visual on the leaders," he reported.

"Mace, you've done everything right so far. Now just stay with them," advised Dex. "Don't pass them yet. It's too early. Join the pack, then hang back and hang tight. Let them know that you have the discipline to wait."

Mace let up on the fuel, falling in behind Taz Nazaryan, Talon, and Akshara Brahma. He *could* give *Trailblazer* more go, if need be. That was encouraging to know.

The track doubled back over Berkeley, and the TURBO-nauts began their descents onto the knot of California free-way. "Choppers incoming," Carson reported. "Be ready for Katana to cut in ahead of you." Mace prepared for land-ing. Aya's green-and-lavender *Lotus* came out of nowhere and touched down on the bridge in front of him. She had a nasty habit of pulling off that stunt! Two more dicers folded their propellers and joined the fray right behind Mace. *Pterodactyl*'s Ariel Pterin almost clipped him. Their sudden appearance was loud and confusing, hard landings in which they almost belly flopped, then half bounced along the freeway as they finished transforming. Mace gathered his focus, punched the gas, and felt the freeway grow steady beneath his tires. He raced along the Embarcadero marginally aware of the screaming crowds. He wasn't able to overtake anyone, but no one got past him, either.

The water-run around Alcatraz was disappointing. Mace's off-the-pier entry was slow. Napoleon outmaneuvered him on the way up through San Pablo Bay. *Chariot* and *Sonar* simply outpowered *Trailblazer*. Mace reentered Sonoma Raceway in tenth place. The leaders pulled away from their pit stops before he ever pulled in.

Mace was losing everything he'd gained! He'd beaten off so many racers—and now they were demanding back their rightful place. The true test of this race was dawning on him: endurance. Resolve. Ten reps of this was going to take . . . *passion.*

He overshot his first pit stop and lost seconds backing into his slot so that the mechanics could replace components, tires, and refill fuel. Nearly half an hour later, at the end of the second rep, he came into the pit far too cautiously, heavy on the brakes, creeping into his stall at the cost of precious seconds.

It happened again after the next rep. "You're letting the world know you're new at this," Dex grumbled from the radio after Mace's *third* botched pit stop.

"I'm lulling them into a false sense of security," Mace tried, wincing. "Fourth time's a charm."

On finishing the fifth rep, Carson thrust a bottle of water at him in the pits. "Halfway done!"

"Still in tenth place!" Mace complained. He guzzled the water and tossed it.

"You're staying close to the leaders. Keep it up."

The eighth rep ended with Mace claiming fourth place. But he got no love from his mustache-stroking crew chief. "Hey, watch the hard landings on the Bay Bridge, okay? You've got multiple reps to go, and the shocks are strained. I can't replace those mid-race."

Mace's confidence suffered with each water entry but grew steadier on the ground and air. During the ninth rep, he flirted with third place, then dropped back to eighth on the San Pablo run. "CRUD!"

But he saw an opportunity.

He came barreling into the pits at full speed, then stopped rapidly on the mark. “Go, go, go!” he shouted to his crew.

“Give me ten extra miles of fuel,” he told Mr. Gerber.

“Why?”

“I’m going to skip the final pit stop.”

Mr. Gerber eyed him hard, thinking. “Bad idea.”

“She can do it. I have the option, right? Legally speaking?”

“There’s nothing in the rules against it.”

“Then do it.”

The chief relayed the order.

The crew scrambled, finished their tasks in lightning speed, and Mace floored the pedal, rocketing off the line. He missed leaping ahead of *Apocalypse* and was forced to fall in behind the leaders like a lowly sixth grader in the lunch line.

Dex came into his ear. “You’re where you need to be. The real race starts now. This is a new animal. No more psychology. It’s all about you and the asphalt. Lean into it and get the job done.”

But Mace held back. The entire rep, he took *Trailblazer* a little easier on the road surfaces. Dex was going insane, but he ignored his wingman’s cries. *I’ve gotta believe in myself.*

Even so, his tires were wearing thin. The extra fuel was heavy. It cost him more time, but the craft held together. He eased onto the road after the final water-to-ground morph and let out his breath. "Now we see what's what." Well over three hours of racing were behind him. He entered the speedway for the last time.

The Pro-Am closed with ten final ground-laps. Mace entered the track in fifteenth place. "This is going to be tough," Dex said.

Mace shook his head. "I'm skipping the pit."

"What?" Dex protested. "You'll never take them if you're bald and they're running fresh! You need fuel."

"All fourteen leaders have stopped for fuel and new tires," reported Mr. Gerber.

"See?" urged Dex. "The only hope you have is outracing them with fresh equipment."

Mace closed his eyes coming around the first turn. He listened to *Trailblazer*, his entire body a seismometer needle, ready to pick up on the slightest warning tremble.

And there it was: a wobble on the front left tire. A thinning bald patch that could definitely blow within the next ten miles of asphalt. The vehicle wanted to tug left. But Mace had put all his chips on the table with this gambit. He had no choice.

"I have to go all in," he said.

Mace gunned it past the crowded pits and kept going. Just like that, he was in first place—and alone.

The crowds! The crowds were going *insane.*

It took four laps for anyone to catch him. By then, he felt his tires would last the final six. But that wobble—he had to ease off the turns a bit. It cost him. Aya blew past him. Then Talon and Taz. Then Cori 'Coriolis' Collins behind the wheel of *Monsoon*. That put him in fifth place. The wobble threatened to unravel. Mace let off the gas. Randall Horseman of *Apocalypse* took advantage. Now he was in sixth.

Even without a final pit stop, he was inevitably falling behind. Dex had been right. Riding on bald tires was going to cost him more than a stop would have.

Dex came on the mic. He sounded glum. "How does it feel?"

"I don't know," Mace said. "I threw the vets for a loop. I'm in good position, better than I was after most reps."

"I hope you're right. No one's succeeded at this for years.

There's a reason, you know."

Yeah, Mace thought. *They're not named Renegade.*

Three laps to go, and he was holding steady in sixth position. Mace exhaled. *Pretend your tires are brand-new.* There was no point in holding back anymore. "Here we go."

He inched ahead of *Apocalypse* on the straightaway and secured his gain by closing off the inner lane as they entered the turn. Veteran Randall Horseman fell farther behind as *Trailblazer's* superior engine outperformed him. Mace was an emotional basket case. Sixth place with three laps to go! He needed third or better to qualify for the Gauntlet Prix!

The four leaders were so far ahead, he didn't see how he could catch them with so little blacktop left.

A wobble. Quivering.

No. There's too much at stake!

The final lap was underway. Mace had closed the distance to the leaders, but the math looked bad. His wheels were furious. He was on *Monsoon*'s tail, locked in a close battle for fifth. But her pilot, Coriolis, wasn't taking chances. He couldn't get around her. She was everywhere.

He knew then, beyond any doubt: crossing the finish line wasn't enough.

He wanted more.

Mace and Coriolis entered the third and final curve, catching Taz Nazaryan, who was too savvy to allow anyone past him. Mace knew the standings were fixed, barring a miracle. Talon was seconds away from a surprise upset victory, Aya only a millisecond behind him, and then TazNaz and Coriolis next, with Mace locked out at fifth place.

Aya was in second. She would be taking a dicer to the Prix!

Another wobble. This one was furious. The thumping became constant, rhythmic.

He could work with the unraveling tire as long as it held a beat, a pattern.

Coriolis found an opening. She took the curve wide in a bid to outgun *Pitchfork* on the outside. Taz veered right to deny her a path forward—leaving the inside lane vulnerable to a suicide bid by Mace. He saw the mistake instantly, made a thousand calculations in his head, and went in for blood.

Rumbling now. But predictable.

"Come on, hold together for ten more seconds."

He guided *Trailblazer* into the narrow gap created by Taz. He won the position! But the checkered flag was close. They were on the final straightaway. His foot was to the floor, every sense in his body focused on *Trailblazer's* purring—and the tortured howl of whatever was left of his front left tire.

He thought she had it in her! Even if the tire blew now, momentum would carry him on through.

But would he cross in third? Or fourth?

Talon and Aya were across the finish line. But it was a three-way tie for third.

Mace risked a glance to the side. Taz was right there. Coriolis clipped him! Taz swerved and corrected. Coriolis had to dodge him. They both fell back! Mace zeroed in on the finish, crossed the line, and shot forward with no one remotely near him.

Mace Blazer let out a shrill cry. Like a flicker of lightning, all in an instant, he had struck, taking third place. He had won a spot in the Gauntlet Prix.

And then his tire blew, and his view of the world turned into a chaotic smear.

CHAPTER THIRTY //////

Mace was at the center of the world's most expensive fidget spinner.

There was nothing he could do to stop the whirling.

The vehicle snagged on the road shoulder, and he flipped. He looked up—or was it down?—saw grass. He was careening into the raceway's open center, and, thank God, not toward a wall.

He flipped again. His seating ballooned, grabbing him tighter than ever. The violent forces tearing at his bones ceased. He looked up—yes, it was up this time. *Trailblazer* had come to a halt on the field, shredded wheels down. Fire trucks were approaching. He popped the spiderwebbed canopy and sprang away from the craft. He fell on shaky legs, then stood. He toppled again, and rose to his knees, waiting for the dizziness to pass.

The crowds were beside themselves. The world was a cauldron of roaring.

Trailblazer. Was the vehicle okay?

Sirens wailed. Flashing yellow lights all over the stadium.

Mace studied the damage. She was in one piece. The canopy was shattered, but that was easy to replace. A few dents. They could afford that. Nothing Mr. Hernandez couldn't handle. Mr. H. was probably watching this from home, already taking notes.

A strange sound filled Mace's ears. Screaming? No. Shouting. Laughter. His crew was celebrating. "Third!" they were chanting. "Third, third, third!"

He heard Carson cry, "And he gets the bronze! He's in the money!"

Mace gulped. Prize money. And he had been tallying up repair tabs in his brain like it was the end of the month and he was out of allowance! They were flush with cash!

Firefighters helped him remain steady on his feet. He was dizzy, and stiff as C-3PO. Even without the crash, three-plus hours of racing, leaning forward and tense the entire time, had made his body angry at him. He scanned the grandstands for his parents as he stumbled to a waiting escort vehicle. He needed them to know he was okay. The megascreens were showing celebrations in three pits. One with red-and-black jumpsuits, one with green-and-lavender jerseys, and a crew dressed in—blue and orange.

That's my *crew.*

And then he saw his parents hugging, crying, cheering. He'd done it. He'd done it the right way. He waved in their general direction. They waved back. Mace retreated below the stadium. The firefighters wanted to test him for a concussion, but he refused treatment. No one could find out his age. A medical exam could wait until later, at the ER, when he would seem like just any kid off the street. The first responders shuffled off, leaving Mace alone in the locker room. A large television fastened to the wall was showing a live broadcast of *TURBOWORLD.* Mace turned on the volume and placed his helmet on the bench beside him while he waited for Dex to arrive.

They were replaying his finish over and over. It looked amazing from an outside angle! And the crash looked . . . *bad*. No. It looked awesome. He laughed.

But Jax Anders landed a heavy blow to his spirits.

The toothy face of *TURBOWORLD* sat at his glass anchor desk, bantering with his co-host, Lee Weisborne. "I've never seen a TURBOnaut all over the map like that. Botching pit stops, horrible timing on the water entries, gaining and losing in the standings."

"You can't just chalk up a showing like that to pure *chance*," Lee argued. "Even taking third takes some skill."

"That's a glowing endorsement. I can throw a dart behind my back and hit the bull's-eye every once in a while. That's got nothing to do with skill. What we saw out there today was recklessness and dumb luck."

"It was audacious. Ambitious. Daring. Those air-laps were flawless. Skipping the last pit? That's the stuff of legend."

"And it almost got Renegade killed." Anders shrugged. "It was a decent air performance. But I'd use the word clueless. If you put a ten-year-old behind the wheel and told them to hit the gas, they'd go fast. Why? Because they don't know to be afraid. This pilot's like Icarus, if you ask me. Flying too close to the sun—like in the myth. It's a matter of time before the wax melts off his wings and he plummets back to Earth."

Dex strode into the room. He saw what Mace was watching and turned off the monitor with a hurried voice command. He scolded Mace. "You shouldn't watch that."

"A ten-year-old?" Mace complained. "What gives? I'm nearly a teenager."

They both laughed. "Are you okay?" Dex asked.

"Stiff. But I'm in one piece."

"What a show!" Dex congratulated him. "You're in the Prix! Come on. We better get you up on the podium. Text your parents first. They're out of their minds."

Dex threw him his phone. Mace scrolled through the recent messages. There were several dozen from the last ten minutes alone. Mace assured Mom and Dad he was fine.

Aya barged into the locker room, eggplant helmet in hand. "I knew it was you!"

"Whoa!" Dex jumped.

Mace gave her a salute. "I think I'm going to live. Thanks for asking!"

Dex hugged her. "We probably shouldn't all be seen together."

"I'm not staying. But . . . why are you helping him, Dex?" Aya pushed away the hug. She had helmet hair, and she combed her fingers absently through it. "He's a cheater. And he's dangerous even when he's not cheating."

"Skipping the pit wasn't illegal!" Mace said.

"No," she reluctantly agreed. "But it was dangerous. Someone really could have been hurt."

She marched off down the underground hallway.

"Aya! Wait!" Mace yelled after her. "You're in more trouble than you realize!"

"As long as you're around, that's true!" she shouted back. She shoved on her helmet and continued up the ramp to the outside world.

The boys watched her go. Mace put on his helmet and they headed aboveground, too. Dex helped him through the crowd. Mace was blinded by the glint of waiting cameras. The mob parted a little. He looked around to discover he was standing on the lowest level of a three-step platform. Talon stood tall on the highest level beside him, and Aya, hidden behind her visor, waved to the crowds from her second-place perch.

Someone had shaken a bottle of sparkling wine and

sprayed it on the victors. Mace wiped the foam away from his mask. Dex spoke into his earpiece. "Straighten up. Wave."

Talon gave the cryptic pilots flanking him each a shoulder squeeze. "Both very impressive out there," he told them. "Why don't you guys take the limelight? No one wants to hear from me today. I'm old news."

He stepped off the podium and dissolved into the crowd.

Aya and Mace now stood side by side. Renegade held out his hand. Katana thought about it, then reached over and accepted the handshake. The crowds loved it, and camera shutters made a sound like a vat of popcorn kernels exploding all at once.

Mace was glad for his flight suit, mask, and gloves.

The purple-tinted surface of Katana's visor studied Mace. They were still shaking hands. "This is for the cameras, slimeball."

Mace ignored her, hurrying, sensing an opportunity to warn her. "Tempest is crazy, Aya. She's up to something bad. I know it."

"I know the danger," she admitted. "But I have a real shot at the Glove, Mace. I can't walk away now."

"Don't trust her or Henryk."

"I don't need your help. I don't want your help. You're just as bad as they are. I can take care of myself."

I'm not like them, Mace wanted to say. But he knew his words meant nothing, not until he could back them up by stopping Tempest by the book.

Aya pulled away and squared her shoulders with the crowd.

They faced a pack of cameras and outstretched phones. A microphone on a boom stick whacked Mace's helmet. Reporters materialized from everywhere all shouting questions all at once.

"Renegade, what were you thinking when you punched through TazNaz's wall?"

"Skipping the pit stop—was that your plan all along?"

"When are you going to take your helmets off for us?"

"Are you the mysterious pilot of trimorpher *Eighty-Three,* from the Philippines?"

Mace finally leaned in on the mics. He spoke with utter resolve. "No. I'm not."

"Katana, you placed in a Prix Qualifier using a dicer. How are you feeling?"

"You're the fifteenth and sixteenth TURBOnauts to

qualify for a shot at this year's Glove. The first amateurs ever to do so. Six of your rivals have won before. Are you ready for the demands of your first Gauntlet?"

Aya stepped forward, ready to answer, but hands seized her shoulders from behind. Tempest, wearing a tailored purple-and-green flight jacket and her larger-than-life sunglasses, placed herself between Aya and the cameras. "My dicer pilot is not taking questions at this time. See you all in Mexico City in two weeks."

The pack of hounds continued shouting questions. "Tempest Hollande, you're a telecommunications giant. Why are you suddenly so involved in TURBO racing?"

Tempest turned back to the reporters. "That's for me to know and for you to find out. But I'll let you in on a little secret. The name Hollande will soon be synonymous with this sport. Mark my words. You're seeing history in the making. Thank you."

Mace followed Tempest into the sloping tunnel leading beneath the stadium. When Aya branched off toward her locker room, Tempest kept marching forward. Mace made his move.

"Don't drag Aya into this," he said.

"Aya's not your concern. She's only here to jack up dicer

stock. It's called diversification." Tempest and Mace locked stares. "Who's helping you?" she demanded in a low growl.

Mace blinked. "No one here but me."

"And I'm the Queen of England," she spat. "Last chance. Who put you up to this?"

"Mickey Mouse," Mace told her.

"Enjoy your third-place finish in a Pro-Am dog and pony show," she spat. "I'm more confident now than ever that letting you go was smart."

Mace looked after her, flabbergasted.

"I offered you everything. Everything. Fame, fortune, a completely reinvented life. You threw it all away." Tempest leaned in on him. "I was going to feed you to my lawyers. I could really twist the dagger, take *everything* from you. But I've changed my mind. Keep your secret. Don't tell me who's backing you. I'm used to having enemies. It's the cost of doing business when you get to my level. We'll settle this on the track. You'll learn then that you're nothing without me."

"Maybe," Mace said. He shook his head. "And maybe it's the other way around—and you're just afraid that even with all your gadgets and money and cheats, you're the one who's really nothing."

Tempest turned her back on him. "This is precious. I can't wait to see you at the Prix. We'll see just how far you get on your own."

Mace's knees suddenly felt wobbly, but he smiled confidently. "I guess we will," he told her as she stormed away. "I guess we will."

///// CHAPTER THIRTY-ONE

Mace stepped out onto the giant plaza feeling small and humbled, surrounded on all sides by towering stone buildings, government headquarters and old hotels. The Zócalo—the ancient Aztec square where the Gauntlet Prix would begin—was perhaps the very heart of Mexico. At the center of the plaza, a green-white-and-red Mexican flag—the largest flag Mace had ever laid eyes upon—rolled on the breeze like an ocean wave.

A hurricane was gathering strength somewhere out in the Caribbean, but Mace would never guess it by the calm blue skies and cartoon clouds overhead.

Around the square, all sixteen Prix-qualifying trimorphers were on display in roadster form. Under heavy surveillance, VIP Pit Access badge holders strolled about. Team jerseys and memorabilia were for sale at every turn. Curbside street vendors sold tacos, tostadas, chicharrónes, tortas, and licuados. In his street clothes, Mace mingled with the crowds. He wandered unnoticed even by the fans decked out in orange-and-blue *Trailblazer* gear. Renegade signs and emblems were everywhere.

He found his way to *Trailblazer*, showed the security crew his team-access badge, and slipped into the tall tent to focus on his final race preparations.

Inside, Dex handed him a tablet. "They're making a couple changes around the Keys to account for the choppy weather tomorrow."

"Is your family safe?" Mace asked.

"I'm not worried for them. Most of these storms lose their steam before they kick into high gear. I'm guessing there will be updates to the route as we go."

Dex turned back to the pile of paperwork he was filling out as Mace took a seat in a folding chair and lost himself studying the Gauntlet Prix routes.

They'd begin in the square, here, in just a few hours, then dart out toward the Gulf of Mexico and the Yucatán Peninsula. For most of the day they'd morph from air to ground to water and back again as they pierced the jungle depths. Then after reaching Cancún, the competition would transition to open ocean, where they'd fly and dive their way to Cuba. That was only day one! They'd overnight in Havana. Stage two would wrap up the following day with a wide swing through the Bahamas and Florida Keys, with a ground race finish along Miami's South Beach.

The tent flap opened wide, flooding the interior with daylight. Mace shielded his eyes. A man in a pushed-down ball cap stood in front of him like a shadow.

"Ahmed!" Mace shot up.

"She knows it's me," he said. "I don't have much time."

Team *Trailblazer*'s security guard burst into the tent and reached for Ahmed. "Hey, buddy, credentials only!"

"It's okay!" Dex came to Ahmed's side. "*¡Está bien!* He's got clearance. We're cool. We're good."

The security guy backed off. "Just doing my job."

"We know. *¡Gracias!*" Dex said as he ushered the guard back out the door. He tied the loose tent flap shut.

Ahmed wasted no time. "Tempest must have paid off someone at the Association. She's knows I'm helping you. She's absolutely furious. She fired me."

"So come work for us," Mace suggested, growing excited.

He shook his head. "I would love to, but you'd be disqualified for partnering with a rival crew. But I have to give you this." He spoke hurriedly. "It's a radio decryption key, set to our team's frequency. Put it on board *Trailblazer.* Use it *only* for safety. You may need to listen in on them, or comm directly with Aya, in case she runs into life-threatening trouble."

"No." Mace crossed his arms. "No cheats."

"This isn't your call," Ahmed told him. "And this isn't for you. It's for Aya and Henryk. For their safety."

Mace frowned, thinking. He shook his head.

"Aya's aware of the risks. But the Prix often takes 'nauts far from immediate help. And that's exactly when Tempest will instruct Henryk to strike. This will be the only way to reach out to Aya if she needs help. I don't want you to use it to gain an advantage. It's only for emergencies."

"Okay," Mace reluctantly agreed. "But I'll only use it if I have to."

"Good." Ahmed sighed. "She's planning something,

Mace. I just can't figure out exactly what it is. She wants Henryk to build a huge lead coming into Miami on day two, at any cost. I mean, huge."

"She wants a sensational win," Dex interpreted.

Ahmed waved his finger at that. "No. There's more to it. She had me build a second *Continuum*. A perfect copy. It's hidden on the Cuban coast."

"Another cheat? Having a backup on hand in case Henryk wrecks?"

"She couldn't pull that off," Dex scoffed. "Cameras will be everywhere. The race is televised by remote drones!"

"Not the ocean runs," Mace noted. "Especially underwater. Those drones only appear every half mile or so."

Ahmed paced the room. "Yes. But to take advantage of those gaps, she'd have to be planning something specific. You can't just dispatch a back-up vehicle *anywhere* and hope for a crash there."

Continuum. Mace racked his brain. Tempest didn't do coincidences. She'd chosen that name for Henryk's trimorpher even though he'd had something else picked out. Why?

"Continuum," he said. "And Infinity." They were intense names. Heavy on physics. Kind of reminded Mace of *Event*

Horizon, and Quasar.

He gasped. "Oh, no. No way."

"What is it?" Dex waited with bated breath.

"I know what she's planning," Mace said. He clenched his jaw, hard. "And we're not going to let her get away with it."

////// CHAPTER THIRTY-TWO

It was official: the hurricane had veered north, projected to shoot far to the east of the Bahamas by tomorrow afternoon. The Gauntlet Prix would proceed as planned. Mace had never doubted this. There was simply too much money on the line to dare let a silly tropical storm interfere with the world's most-watched sporting extravaganza.

Mace was secure in his smart cushioning, going over his countdown checklist while Carson and Mr. Gerber conducted final inspections. The roadsters were lined up in pairs along José María Pino Suárez Boulevard, parked parallel beside the steep bleachers erected in front of the Palacio Nacional. *Trailblazer* occupied slot number fourteen in row seven. To his left was Katana, and to his right, the stands. Beyond *Lotus* was the expanse of the Zócalo, empty save for the giant Mexican flag erect at its center. Two TURBOnauts were behind Mace in positions fifteen and sixteen: *Apocalypse*'s Randall Horseman, wearing his old Golden Glove, and Leon "Napoleon" Dubois, piloting the crimson-and-slate-gray *Guillotine*, who had qualified for six of the last seven Prix without ever placing.

Mace eyed the beautiful gold-and-silver *Continuum* directly in front of him. Henryk was visible as a silhouette behind the canopy, making his final vehicle checks.

Mace glanced at his radio display. One push of a button and he could toggle over to Henryk and Aya, listen in to their comms with Tempest. But only if he had to—and only toward the end, tomorrow, approaching Miami.

That's when Tempest would spring into action, executing her grand conspiracy. Mace knew it. He would be ready.

Dex spoke to him over one of his displays. Dex was already in Havana at their team headquarters. "I just got a text from your parents," he said. "They've landed in Miami."

"Good to hear." Mace's mom and dad had never had passports before and were unable to get them rushed in time for the Gauntlet. But the finish line in Florida was the best place for him to meet up with them anyway. "Tell them I'll be there faster than anyone else."

Dex grinned. "That's the spirit. Will do."

"How's the weather holding up?"

"The storm has stalled out way east, beyond Puerto Rico. You're going to have pretty rough seas coming into Cuba today, but the final word is we're still a go."

Mace felt a familiar prerace flutter of nerves punch his stomach. In five minutes, he'd be airborne, the eyes of the world on him, the safety of his mates and the integrity of this whole sport in the balance.

"This is good news for us, Mace. The skimmers are in for rough stretches. And you're a quick thinker. You can roll with the changing conditions better than these old dogs."

An announcement went out over the loudspeakers, echoing throughout the Zócalo. "Ladies and gentlemen, *damas y caballeros*, start your engines!" The trimorphers fired up, and the roar of each roadster filled the ancient Aztec square like a volcanic eruption. Mr. Gerber scurried off the starting line clutching his clipboards.

Carson lingered. He *signed* to Mace. "Good luck." He looked so proud. "Make all M-O-R-P-H-S matter."

Mace's jaw dropped. He laughed. "Thank you," he signed back.

"Hey," barked Dex. "You're doing it again. Ignition. Now."

Mace flicked the roadster on as the grand marshal waved the green flag. Peeling tires screeched over the roar of the engines. The air filled with smoke, and roadsters in front of *Trail-blazer* pulled away. Carson bolted for shelter. Mace watched, in a trance, as *Lotus*, *Guillotine*, and then *Radioactive* disappeared around his left flank! The Gauntlet Prix had begun.

"Ouch," Mace said. He'd already been passed! He touched the gas, and *Trailblazer* came to life. Her joyful growl beneath his seat, emanating up through him to rattle his rib cage, filled him with fire.

The sixteen racers made a wide lap around the Zócalo, then spiraled inward for another, tighter lap. Tire smoke filled the square like steam in a boiling vat. After a winding sprint to the center flagpole, the only exit would be straight up, giving expensive-ticket holders an unforgettable show before the trimorphers lifted skyward and bolted from Mexico City on their marathon dash toward Cuba, the Bahamas, the Florida Keys, and ultimately Miami.

Mace was in last place, but he was inches away from Randall Horseman's bumper. He watched the leading racers spiral inward while sharply drifting, as if being drawn into a vortex. *Iron Dragon* was first to reach the flagpole and hit the launch ramp. *Untouchable*, *Pterodactyl*, and *Carpe Diem* sprouted helicopter blades, enjoying the best maneuverability for their tight, upward climb. The effect was a metal tornado as the vehicles swarmed upward, dodging the luffing Mexican flag before slingshotting east toward the Gulf of Mexico.

Mace veered inward, reached the launch ramp, and morphed to air.

As he did, barely yet airborne, *Guillotine* and *Apocalypse* collided in front of him! They fell out of the sky, out of the Prix. Mace shot forward, up, circling wide of the explosion and the ejected pilots. The flag had shifted direction suddenly, snapping *Guillotine*'s rotors like a whip, sending Dubois caroming into the next vehicle. Mace exhaled. He was supposed to be in Horseman's position, had he started on time, and he would have crashed instead.

His late jump off the line had saved him.

Thanks, Gerbs! he thought.

The drama of the opening was forgotten in the slog toward the Yucatán. For an hour, Mace patiently gained on the rest of the pack. When he reached the Gulf of Mexico, he was exactly where he wanted to be, in eighth place behind hometown hero Darwín Maldonado of *Evolución,* and South African juggernaut Trevor Bosha, piloting *Midnight Sun*. Beyond them, *Iron Dragon, Pitchfork* and the all-woman cast of leaders piloting *Untouchable*, *Blacksmith*, *Pterodactyl*, and *Castle.*

Aya wasn't far behind Mace. Henryk was several slots farther back. *Biding his time,* Mace guessed. *I know he'll be coming.*

Underwater in the Gulf, he overtook *Blacksmith.* Bethany Ironsides had switched owners and sponsors three times in the last four years. Her homelessness in the sport was a drag on her.

And when he reached the first jungle stretches west of the Yucatán, he finally caught Akshara Brahma. She was a study in perfect execution. Her morphs were flawless. Her pace was steady—but also predictable. Mace could read her like a book. She took an inside curve the way a top bot on the simulator would. And Mace drifted wide around her just as he used to back at the Boulder arcade.

Bosha was Mace's next focus. He inched up on *Midnight Sun*, eventually leaving him behind. And then, of course, there were Ariel Pterin, Talon, Taz Nazaryan, and Darwín Maldonado, visible ahead in Mace's sights, but on the top of their game.

"You're right on track," Dex praised him. "Keep it up."

Mace pushed the gas and drove on.

The fifty-mile-long underwater stretch of Laguna de Términos west of the Yucatán was shallow and smooth. Mace held the line, doing everything right, letting the power beneath the hood of *Trailblazer* do the lion's share of the work.

"Storm's building again," Dex reported. His tone hinted at genuine trouble. "Turning west. They're throwing the word 'hypercane' around."

Mace's stomach sank, not out of fear, but disappointment. "Figures," he said. "These things seem to follow you around."

"I wish that were funny," said Dex.

The TURBOnauts were a bit spread out from each other,

but Mace wasn't letting himself get complacent. The Yucatán jungle was next up. The race would tighten there.

Iron Dragon grabbed the advantage off the next pit stop before the road race toward Cancún. In roadster mode, the rivals coalesced into a tighter line, blowing past crumbling Mayan pyramids buried under centuries of choking vines. This was anybody's checkered flag. Mace cut Aya off, darting forward to overtake her on a downhill drift. She spun out and ran off the shoulder, then stopped, facing the wrong direction.

The road transitioned from what seemed like a green trench into a tunnel—the overhead jungle canopy arched over the course. *Trailblazer*'s tires gripped the road but squealed their annoyance as g-forces spiked.

Continuum unleashed a burst of sudden speed, disappearing around a distant bend. Mace's eyes narrowed behind his visor. Was Henryk giving him the slip?

"No, you don't," Mace growled through clenched teeth. He primed the compression coils and pressed his foot down on the pedal.

He leaned into the curve, throttled to full power, and then tackled the straightaway through a marshy lowland rainforest.

They curved, and curved again, flying blindly along the tight green slit between jungle walls. He passed *Pterodactyl, Avalanche*, and *Carpe Diem.*

The race entered the city of Cancún. Spectators lined every roadway, shoulder to shoulder, several people deep. Mace nailed the mark at his pit stop, fueled up, replaced his tires and transformer modules, and blazed away down the beachside boulevard teeming with fans in bathing suits and bikinis. He maintained his slot in the standings, just behind Henryk.

The path opened up. Finally, ahead of his rival, Mace could make out the launch ramp. *My favorite part,* he thought.

"You've got *Lotus* on your tail, half a mile back," said Dex.

He hadn't realized Aya was so close behind. Of course she would have recovered from his nudge a while ago.

Iron Dragon was already airborne, visible as a shrinking red-black missile. *Continuum* launched into the sky and morphed, wings appearing. Henryk spiraled as he rose and, like that, was gone into the blue.

Mace hovered his finger over the transformer toggle and closed his eyes. *Trailblazer* crossed onto the ramp and tipped upward. Mace felt the change of angle in his marrow. The front wheels passed beyond the ramp edge and came free of the ground. “Now!” he hollered to himself, opening his eyes and pounding the knob. His timing was flawless.

Trailblazer folded up its tires, extended its wings and dorsal fin, and pierced forward into the sky without losing one microsecond of inertia.

The jungle canopy was suddenly far below him, a disheveled green shag carpet. The afterburner roared, and Mace felt an unexpected joy as he drew closer to his rival.

Dex came on. “Uh, crazy news, Mace.”

“What’s going on?” he asked.

“Storm’s getting stronger—and fast. The Association is shortening the race. Checkered flag will be in Havana. Today.”

“Seriously? That changes everything!” Mace exclaimed.

Just then, he felt a muffled shockwave pass through his bones.

Iron Dragon was plummeting, billowing smoke as it went. Talon had deployed a chute. He guided himself toward the jungle floor.

Henryk must have used debris to shred *Iron Dragon*’s engine, a move he had perfected on Mace.

"*Iron Dragon*'s out of the Prix!" he reported to Dex.

"What? What happened?"

Continuum was a dot in the distance, gaining speed.

"Henryk," Mace said. "It's starting. Tempest has ordered him to start clearing out the competition."

Just like Mace had known she would.

CHAPTER THIRTY-THREE //////

The TURBOnauts raced over the jungle canopy, doubling back for an aerial flyby of Cancún. The white beach and azure blue of the shallow Caribbean coast came back into view. The city of Cancún interrupted the emerald treetops. Beyond that, the rainforest expanse of the ancient Mayan empire stretched off to the south, and the deep ocean churned ahead.

"You can't let him break away, Mace."

"I won't."

"Can you see the storm on the horizon?" Dex asked.

Dark clouds masked the east. "That's a big fat affirmative," Mace answered.

"Everyone's adjusting their tactics," Dex told him. "It's gonna get frantic. If you're right about Tempest, she'll be scrambling."

The race continued, and soon *Continuum* was in Mace's sights.

If he could force Henryk to make an error now, there'd be no time for him—or for Tempest—to try shady tactics later. *Be as aggressive as you can,* Mace told himself. *Shake him up.*

He moved in.

Mace rolled and lifted, only increasing speed, closing the distance to *Continuum* so that the tip of *Trailblazer* turned red with heat against Henryk's exhaust.

Dex was panicky. "You're too close, Mace! Drop back! What're you doing?"

Mace didn't slow down. He dropped low instead, hugging his opponent's wake. He resisted the temptation to overtake Henryk. The point here was to annoy him.

A large piece of metal came at Mace's windshield like a missile. "Not this time!" Mace cried. He rolled away, dodging the debris. He roared, victorious. Henryk had spent his move. Audiences would grow suspicious if that happened again. But Mace would have to stay vigilant. Henryk had to have other tricks up his sleeve.

They turned as if interlocked in a graceful ballet move. Another hoop neared. Henryk dipped, forcing Mace to drop. If he missed entering the hoop, he'd be docked precious time at the finish! But Mace was in control. He flipped around, shot up and tried to mount *Continuum*. Henryk expected this and rose to match the countermaneuver. Mace ducked instead, won back his low ground—and pushed Henryk upward at the last second so that *Continuum* nearly overshot the hoop from above!

It was a close call, but they both made it through the halo.

The Cancún audiences were rearview history. The wave-wracked ocean filled Mace's view.

"Water entry in T minus fifteen seconds," warned Dex. "Drop back! You'll tear to pieces if you enter in his wake."

Yes, but . . . Mace couldn't give up ground. He thought quickly. *I'll draw parallel, enter at the same time, maybe just ahead of him.* "Let's see if he likes feeling *my* wake!"

Incredibly, Mace punched the throttle as the ocean

surface neared. He swung to the side and drew level with *Continuum*. This was going to work!

"Mace! Don't forget to—"

Morph! His chest exploded with sudden fear. He extended his thumb over the air-to-water switch. The sea was a concrete wall at these speeds.

He entered the water, saw the ocean floor screaming up at him—

He hit the shallow seabed violently. Freezing water entered the cockpit, but he was prepared for it. *This feels familiar.* He knew right where to find the pressure compensator and pounded it.

The cockpit drained. He glanced around himself, peered out the canopy. A tiger shark drifted past, considered him briefly, and disappeared back into the blue. He restarted the turbine and got into gear.

Lotus arrived, a muffled *whoomf* marking Aya's smooth entrance into the Caribbean. Another TURBO craft punctured the water, jostling *Trailblazer*. It was *Untouchable*.

The gamble to force Henryk into a costly error had backfired. "No, no, no!" Mace barked. "Henryk will pick you off, one at a time!"

He urged *Trailblazer* to gather speed. *I've got to get back in the mix!*

"Get in there! This is the final stretch. One hundred and fifty miles before landfall. It's still possible for you to win this thing, Mace. Just work your way up to Aya and Akshara and stay a step ahead of Henryk."

I can do this. Mace closed his eyes, throttled up, and reentered the fray.

The race across the ocean was a series of glorified dolphin leaps—water, air, water, air—and the gathering storm was forcing course changes all the time. Mace took advantage of the rough conditions, closing the gap with the leaders. He stayed ahead of—and broadened his lead over—Taz, who was having trouble with all the rerouting. Drone-powered hoops were repositioned by Prix technicians, making flight paths longer and contact with the water shorter.

Mace was flexible. He adapted quickly and continued gaining.

Finally, he clawed his way to within striking distance of *Untouchable*. He gained on her, coming in from the left, then the right, then the left again. He overtook Akshara Brahma, entering the next water segment with no one but *Lotus* and

Continuum in front of him. And soon enough, *Trailblazer* muscled up behind Aya, riding her wake and finding even more speed. The water was downright choppy. Mace realized he could ride Aya's eddies indefinitely, save fuel, bank power for an eventual slingshot at the right moment. He could keep an eye on her this way. This was his ticket to Cuba, and ultimately, the Prix checkered flag.

Mace and Aya both shot past *Pterodactyl,* leaving her far behind. *Continuum* was all that remained. The morph to ground on Cuba's choppy shore was approaching, and the three youngest 'nauts in the sport were dueling for first with no one else in the rearview.

Mace and Aya caught up to Henryk but stayed just far enough away to avoid any dirty tricks he might try to pull. Mace decided he would make his move on the surface, where cameras could record any of Henryk's attempts to cheat.

All three of them. First, second, and third! *Iron Dragon* would probably still be in the mix if there hadn't been foul play, but still, Mace realized something. It made him kind of sad. Tempest had done a really good job of finding them, equipping them, and training them. If she had groomed all of them to their full potential, she would have been remembered as a legend. She would have ushered in a new era for the sport, proving that younger racers had what it took to go the distance.

Instead, she had only wanted to take credit for a cheap win.

Mace figured out that it was no coincidence that he—and Tempest's other three finalists—were all nearly the same size as her.

Tempest had been planning her treachery from the very beginning.

He was sure he had discovered the truth. Her scheme seemed obvious to him now. So where was she? The finish line had been changed. Tempest would need to make her move soon, or—

A sudden vibration snapped him out of his angry realization. "Um, wow," he said nervously. *That feels like a . . .*

PROJECTILE DETECTED

TAKE EVASIVE ACTION

Trailblazer's displays flashed red.

Mace watched in horror as a torpedo barreled through the water toward him and Henryk and Aya.

///// CHAPTER THIRTY-FOUR

The warnings alone wouldn't have saved him, but it turned out that dodging the police missile over Denver had been all the training he'd needed. Mace initiated a lateral roll. He pulled up and back, over *Continuum*'s canopy.

The missile sailed below him . . . and detonated on *Continuum*'s nose.

Mace was fine, but Henryk's turbine seized, grinding to a halt. The craft went askew, pitching forward, sinking. Strangely, there was no evidence of damage to *Continuum*'s hull.

EMP! Mace thought. An electromagnetic pulse—not a

missile but a blast of electric noise.

Concerned, he and Aya both slowed.

Then, he felt, more than he could see, *Pitchfork* skim overhead. *Untouchable* bulleted by in a wide arc, steering clear of this whole mess. Both would touch down on the Cuban coast and duke it out into Havana with a clear advantage.

"No!" Mace ground his teeth.

Ahead in the murky distance, a second *Continuum* pulled into action, turning in a wide arc to join the chase.

"I knew it!" Mace cried.

"What's going on?" Dex asked. "The live broadcast lost you all. It's really rough up top."

"She's here," Mace said. "She's already disabled Henryk."

"Tempest?!" said Dex. "You were right about her!"

"I wish I wasn't," grumbled Mace. "It's time I listen in, just to make certain."

He hesitated for just a second, then punched a light display that would allow him to intercept all of Tempest Hollande's comms.

Sure enough, she sounded in his ear, unaware that she was being overheard. "Henryk was supposed to have a much larger lead at this point. I'll adjust, though. We're going to surface. Fall in line behind me; keep Mace off my tail. Is that clear?"

Aya was beside herself with revulsion. "What? No!"

"Hiya, Aya!" Mace interjected loudly.

"Mace!" Tempest spat. "Get off our channel!"

"My friends call me Mace. You can call me Renegade."

They all built speed, continuing to torpedo through the water on course for the Cuban shore. The storm surge on the surface rocked their hulls back and forth in unison.

"Someone PLEASE explain!" Aya growled.

"You want the short answer or the long answer?" Mace began.

Tempest cut him off. "You stay out of this, you little brat. I made you. And I'm going to end you as well."

"I'll keep it quick, then," Mace decided.

"Just . . . PLEASE," Aya snapped. "What's going on?"

"Tempest has taken Henryk out with an electronic bomb. She's planning to use his lead to cross the finish line in first place—as *herself*."

Aya growled, suddenly understanding. "She'll take the podium, accept the Glove, remove her helmet . . . and reveal herself to the world . . ."

Mace imitated a sportscaster. "Infinity *is* Quasar!

Tempest Hollande! The oldest 'naut to ever claim the Glove! And she did it despite missing an eye! What a comeback story!"

"Jax Anders and his cronies would gobble that story up!" Aya agreed.

"She wants to ruin TURBO racing. Turn it into a demolition derby with all sorts of foul play and gimmicks. She'll corner the market on all of it. Fit new TURBO racers with weaponry. Then fit another new generation with counterattacks. Make a billion dollars. Does that sound about right, Tempest?"

"Mind your own business, Renegade."

"But more than that: she's never stopped wanting that Glove . . . for *herself*," Mace concluded. "Wearing the Glove would give her a winning message that only she could deliver. But she can't pull off a win on her own. Not with one eye and no depth perception. So she hired us."

"But why us?" Aya demanded.

"Because we all share the same height and weight," Mace figured. "And because adults don't use the sims, I bet."

"She thought we'd roll over and play along," added Aya.

"You're all wrong!" cried Tempest, but she never offered

a different explanation.

"What about Henryk?" Aya asked. "He's sinking!"

"He's not your concern," Tempest told her. "After the storm passes through here, no one will ever know what happened to him."

"He's going to die down there if we don't do something," said Mace. "He doesn't deserve to end up as shark bait."

"I'll rescue him," Aya said coolly.

She turned *Lotus* around.

"AYA!" Tempest screamed. "What are you doing?!"

"It's over, Tempest. I didn't sign up for this. I'm through listening to you."

"You have a second-place Gauntlet Prix finish locked up. In a *dicer!* You want to lose everything—to save *Henryk*?"

Mace gritted his teeth. "I'll fetch him, Aya. She's right. You go."

"No, Mace," she said, descending. "Beat her—but do it right! I know you can."

"I'm finished with all of you," Tempest spat. "You're leaving me no choice. You'll all go down for this."

"But, Aya, what about—"

"I can take care of myself." Aya's voice cut in and out,

grew steady. “Go! Beat her! Win the Glove!”

“Dream on,” Tempest sneered. “You never got any storm training. I’ll crush you between here and Havana.”

Not this time, Mace thought. He manually overrode the limitation Mr. Gerber had put on his Pegasus X-90, Class D, and rammed the turbine throttle to max.

“If you’re so sure, then what are you afraid of?” he dared Tempest.

“I’ve never been afraid of anything in my life. That’s the difference between sitting at the table and being on the menu.”

Mace laughed. “You’re on,” he said. “Let’s race.”

///// CHAPTER THIRTY-FIVE

Mace reached the sloping, shallow floor of the Cuban coast. *Trailblazer* and *Continuum II* rocked back and forth in the rip currents, their bellies scraping coral. The gathering storm's wrath was waiting for them the moment they surfaced.

Undertows and riptides tore in every direction. But eventually Mace found the rhythm of the dance, building power until he shot out of the water and morphed into a roadster. Mace peeled out on the sand, speeding into a fierce rain and wind after Tempest.

The coastal highway was a long stretch of racetrack,

empty except for Renegade and Quasar. The sport's oldest and youngest 'nauts dueled. Mace accelerated into the gale-force winds, heavy rain hammering his canopy, blotting out his vision. The howling gusts scrambled his ability to feel the road, so he was forced to keep his speed in check.

Tempest stayed several lengths ahead of him—for now.

Fortunately, his fresh tires from the Cancún pit stop were street-ready with deep treads. Still, Mace hydroplaned repeatedly—but he was a fast study in bad-weather racing. Quickly, he learned how to anticipate the rough patches, and to move with the wind instead of against it.

Mace was far more worried about fuel than anything else. Tempest had a full tank, and he was one hundred and fifty miles past his last fill-up.

In the blasting sand and rain, Mace lost sight of *Continuum II*—but he could still reach out to Quasar over the local comm.

"The four of us kids would have dominated the finish line today," said Mace. "Without your cheats. You would have been a legendary coach. Immortal. Now look at you."

No answer.

Mace's heartbeat quickened, his vision tunneled. Never

had he felt so at one with his vehicle. There was no gap between thought and action. The blurry canopy was but a nuisance, and Mace accelerated through the storm as if he were out for a scenic drive.

"As soon we pass the flag, I'll have you locked away," Tempest finally replied. "Mystery of the stolen *Event Horizon* solved. You'll be finished."

Whatever. That moment was a million years away. All Mace cared about right now was winning the Glove.

He remembered Dex and switched his radio over. "Yo! Caballero?"

A crackle came to Mace's ears. "Mace, what's happening out there?"

"Oh, you know, just racin' . . . You hear from Aya?"

"Yeah, she has Henryk in tow. Coast Guard's closing in."

"Good." Mace sighed.

Steering through the squall, Renegade watched Quasar try to morph to air, growing wings, lifting off the ground, only to be pummeled by the wind and rain, losing control, and slamming back down to earth in roadster form. He switched to her comm line. "You can't just airlift your way out of this," he said, watching her like a hawk.

Mace waited for a chance to go airborne himself, but the storm owned the sky. He tried and was smacked down as if by a giant flyswatter. There was simply no way to get liftoff in this maelstrom.

"A ground race it is."

He pumped the gas, drifted the curves like a pro, and found his own rhythm on the road despite the conditions.

But Tempest wouldn't give way. She answered his every move. He couldn't squeeze by her.

Then a tight bend came out of nowhere. Mace watched in horror as Tempest lost the roadway, dipped from view below a cliff. He thought he'd just seen her die—until she rose as an aircraft a moment later. He slowed, respected the turn without losing contact, and eased into a half drift. As he gathered back speed, Tempest settled on to the pavement, still ahead of him.

She sped down a hill with Mace right on her. The bridge at the bottom had been washed away. The banks had crumbled into the brown water. Tempest bulleted over the water's edge, morphing into a sub, taking the flash flood like a skipping stone in three successive bounces. She hit the far side of the highway as a roadster, her tires grabbing the asphalt and accelerating her up the next hill. Mace followed suit, flawlessly executing the same sequence of rapid morphs. A fallen tree bobbing in the water struck his hull, jostling him, but he recovered his grip on the wheel and corrected his steering in time to catch the pavement.

Pitchfork and *Untouchable* materialized out of nowhere up ahead, racing up the middle of the road at a cautious pace through the pelting rain. Tempest swung to their left at full blast, showering them with a wall of water. Mace veered past to the right, nearly pushing them off the road.

"You just passed the remaining leaders, Mace," Dex confirmed. "The only thing between you and the finish line is Tempest Hollande."

"She won't let me pass, Dex! She's tougher than I thought!"

"You're Renegade. *You're* tougher than *she* thinks. You can do this!"

They passed a landing checkpoint, where they would have touched down as roadsters for the final approach had the weather been different. Mace gritted his teeth. Overtaking Tempest with a daring air leap was out of the question now. Rules stipulated that they remain roadsters with wheels on the ground from here until the finish.

They blew through ramshackle towns. Die-hard fans braved the storm to watch them hydroplane through the villages. And then the countryside disappeared, replaced with a constant blur of high-rise buildings and packed crowds. They were entering the outskirts of Havana. The whole of Cuba, it seemed, was on hand to witness the epic chase. They might have been drenched to the bone, but they were still fired up.

Mace loved it.

Whatever his future held—no matter how much trouble Tempest was going to cause him—Mace owed these fans an honest victory.

He made his move, hammering the pedal to the floor.

Tempest veered, blocking his path.

"Shoot!" *What's it gonna take to squeeze by her?!*

They blazed past crumbling baseball stadiums, tall statues, high-rise apartment complexes, and hotels. The billboards, large and rattled by storm winds, displayed solid colors, bearded figures in green berets, and simple Spanish phrases:

Esta revolución es hija de la cultura.

Son las ideas las que iluminan al mundo.

Crowds lined every sidewalk, cheering loudly enough for him to hear.

The boulevard narrowed, boxed on the sides with stone offices and bleachers. *Too narrow!* If passing had been beyond difficult earlier—it seemed impossible now.

They pressed on. *Trailblazer* gave a jerk and a stutter. Mace looked at his fuel gauge. It was bottomed out. He couldn't believe it: he was on fumes!

Continuum II screamed over the asphalt, never slowing, plowing through standing pools and spraying up walls of water. She'd lose control, compensate with her drift fins, find the line. Mace chased her down, risking a burst of speed, and hydroplaned right into the back of her.

He flipped to her comm channel. "Oh, hi. There you are," he said.

"Back off!" she snarled in his ears.

Mace did back off, but just a hair. A half mile ahead, the tattered checkered banner whipped ferociously in the torrential winds. A gust threatened to pick *Continuum II* off the ground. Tempest used a drift fin again to stabilize.

Mace wondered: had she left the ground right then? Would she be disqualified for that? *That won't do,* he thought.

"I have to win by winning, not through a technicality."

A crazy vision entered his head. He drew in a deep breath.

He knew what to do.

Rules stipulate that you need at least two wheels on the ground during any ground terrain.

Maintaining a steady grip with one hand, Mace gauged the howling winds. He cut to the left. Quasar answered by blocking him. He swerved to the right, and so did she. His free hand typed commands into the forward display, and he punched morph-to-air.

But only his right wing extended.

He gave *Trailblazer* a mad burst of speed. The Pegasus engine revved to 100 percent. The vehicle turned on its side, the extended wing rising over the top of *Continuum II*'s canopy. His own canopy remained inches from grazing the safety fencing facing the bleachers. There was a backfire.

Out of gas.

Nothing to do now but coast. He cut through the fierce winds like a dart, half aircraft, half roadster, his two *left* wheels always against asphalt.

Tempest wavered, struggling to control her roadster. Her stabilizing fins came up again. Mistake. The drag slowed her down. Not much. But just enough.

Mace overtook her. Without a fraction of a second to spare, he retracted his wing, and slammed down on all fours in front of her. He slowed. But it was too late for Quasar to retake him.

He whipped across the finish line.

Crowd roar rose to a howl, drowning out the winds.

Mace drew in a starved breath.

He'd taken the checkered flag.

The Glove was his.

CHAPTER THIRTY-SIX //////

Mace hit the brakes.

Tempest barreled into him from behind. His smart cushioning absorbed the forces as they came to a halt, hydroplaning and bouncing off the boulevard fencing like bowling balls on a bumpered lane.

"You cheated!" Tempest said, sneering over the comm.

"I never cheated," he replied. "I always had at least two wheels on the ground. Rules don't specify which two wheels they need to be. Look it up."

"You look it up. I'll send you a rulebook in prison, after

I explain to the cops that you stole *Event Horizon* from the Boulder Airport."

Mace felt a sudden stab of fear. *Continuum II* rested off-kilter beside him. He studied Tempest's hull for damage as Tempest stirred within. She lifted the visor of her golden helmet, peering out of her canopy at him through the downpour with nothing but blind rage.

Sirens wailed from somewhere beyond the street's canyon walls, growing nearer.

"Some parting advice for you," Tempest offered across their dedicated comm. "Keep your mouth shut. Anything you say will only come back to haunt you."

Anything you say . . .

The pounding of his heart in his ears fell suddenly silent.

Mace laughed his relief. "I can prove you're behind all this!"

"Prove what?" she ruthlessly continued. "That I hired you and the others to win for me? That the payouts you all received came from my accounts? You don't think I covered my tracks? You're going to claim that I swapped places with Henryk? Even if he survives, I'll just say *he* tried to replace *me*. He'll never be able to prove that I didn't pilot *Continuum* all along. It's your word against mine. Trust me, I've covered it all."

"Keep talking," Mace replied. "You're just making this easier." He patted his dash so that she could see what he was referring to.

Tempest glowered at him across the distance. "No," she said.

"It's all here. Every word you've spoken since zapping Henryk. All comms are recorded. For training purposes. Right? I believe Ahmed taught me that."

A pair of Cuban police cruisers came into view from around the corner. Mace could hear above the roar of the storm a message reaching out to them by bullhorn: "Remain securely in your cockpits. We'll retrieve you one by one and get you both to safety. We'll start with the closest of you—the winner."

Mace laughed. "That would be me, wouldn't it?"

"Damn you, Mace Blazer," Tempest seethed. "I gave you everything. I was so good to you. Don't you see—"

She stopped. The officers were approaching, now, holding their arms out against the gale forces. Mace encouraged her on. "Keep talking, keep talking," he told her.

She shook her head. There was a long pause. They studied each other across the empty, rain-swept avenue. Behind Tempest, a bleacher succumbed to the wind, tearing away from its mooring and sliding onto the road. The spectators cried out in alarm. *Trailblazer* and *Continuum II* were rocked by the same gust. The officers might have blown away if they hadn't been crouched low to the ground.

The audiences sitting in *all* the bleachers up and down the boulevard got the message: it was time to scram. The storm was getting stronger. They filed away in a hurry.

"I'm grateful you gave me the chance to race. I love this sport," Mace said. "I know I wouldn't be here if it wasn't for you."

Untouchable and *Pitchfork* turned a distant corner and were now visible gunning it up the long boulevard, jostling for third place.

"I'm not going to jail, Mace. I can afford to choose my fate. I told you about the cost of doing business once. Now you know what it buys."

"But the things you win—how can they matter, if you can never stand to lose?"

"You could have been great, Mace," she told him. "We

could have done this year after year. Traveling the globe. Rich. And now here you are. You'll never be allowed to race again. You're an underage nobody."

"Actually, I'm the world's youngest Gauntlet Prix winner."

Tempest revved her engine, startling the police officers, who were still hunkered down on their approach, their uniform ponchos billowing madly. "I'll see you around, Renegade. Or maybe I won't." Mace watched helplessly as Tempest reversed and executed a tight one-eighty.

Incredibly, even wrecked, *Continuum II* launched to air and rose up over the cityscape. The screaming winds took hold of her.

"No!" Mace hollered, terrified.

Tempest disappeared in the grim, gray haze of violent sky above.

////// CHAPTER THIRTY-SEVEN

The awards ceremony was delayed overnight until the storm had moved on. Cleanup was only just beginning. The Gerbers were en route from Mexico, but Mace's parents remained stuck in Florida.

Mace sat quietly beside Dex, against the outside wall of the Habana Paradiso Hotel. Dex twirled his cowboy hat like a hoop as they people-watched. Reporters were everywhere, tracking down leads in a massive story they were only just beginning to comprehend.

The aftermath of the hypercane was prominent. Large

palm fronds and tree branches blocked streets and sidewalks. One old oak had uprooted entirely, smashing parked muscle cars along the path of its fall. Lawns were flooded. Trash had blown about and snagged on hedgerows and statues. The cobbled streets and footpaths were caked in mud, and power lines were down.

But the town square was brilliantly decorated. Pennants hung from crisscrossing strings, sporting *Trailblazer*'s colors and logo. Maroon-and-gold TazNaz memorabilia, along with *Untouchable*'s colors of orange, white, and green, were also strung around the plaza. TURBO Association banners were on display everywhere the news cameras might turn. The brilliant blue sky held few clouds, and the sun cast a pleasant warmth over the impatient crowds. Technicians had just finished constructing the dais where the Glove would be presented. Reporters and fans were already gathering around the stage.

Cutting through it all, a beautiful red carpet. At one end was the stage and the tri-level podiums upon which the first three finishers would take their bows. At the other end, a heavily guarded table—Mace thought of it as an altar—hosting this year's Golden Gauntlet. It was already etched with the name Renegade. Mace kept his distance, waiting for the moment when it would come to him.

Yesterday, Mace had stayed hidden beneath his helmet until he had found privacy in his hotel suite.

When he went outside, no one ever suspected he might be Renegade.

"I'm right here," Mace presently offered under his breath as one reporter hurried by, yelling on her phone that she had no leads as to Renegade's whereabouts.

"Hey, Dex," Mace asked. "I saw lots of billboards as I was coming into the city. One of them said, *'Esta revolución es la hija de la cultura.'* You know what that means?"

"Sure." Dex thought for a moment. "It probably best translates to, 'Revolution is in our blood.'"

"Ah," Mace said.

And then from around a corner, Aya strode over. She sat down beside them against the hotel wall. She was dressed in plain clothes just like the boys.

"Congrats," she simply said.

"That Glove over there belongs to all three of us," he told her.

"Okay," Aya said. "I get custody on Tuesdays. And Leap Days."

Dex laughed.

Mace raised an eyebrow. "So, um, are we talking to each other again?"

She allowed her eyes to open up a bit for him. The warmth he saw there made him feel dizzy.

"The way I grew up," she explained, "my parents never paid attention to me. I tried everything to get them to notice—I was perfect at soccer, school, even *chadō*, the art of preparing and presenting Japanese tea. Same with the TURBO sim. I thought if I was the best at something they'd care a little."

"Okay," said Mace, suddenly feeling uncomfortable. "Explains a lot, I guess."

"You taught me a lesson yesterday."

"Really?"

She nodded. "I never raced for the joy of it. If you race only to be perfect, only to get someone else to notice, you never learn how to love the sport. But you, Mace—you love this sport."

"I almost killed you!" he stammered.

"Yeah, but even that was about passion. It was misguided, but I get that you were being fooled. We all were."

A short silence followed. Mace hated silences, and this was one for the record books. He started to squirm. Aya took his hand in hers and gave it a squeeze.

Mace looked down at their interlaced fingers, shocked. He caught her stare, the warmth in her eyes, and then pulled away like a reflex and regretted it almost instantly.

"How's your family?" Aya asked Dex. "They okay in the D.R.?"

Dex's smile vanished. "I'm not sure," he answered. "Haven't been able to get through to anyone. I talked to my sister in New York. She seems to think everyone's safe. Judging by the damage down here, it'll probably be a few days before we really know."

"You can pop over there in *Trailblazer,*" Mace joked. "Check on them yourself."

"Yeah," Dex quipped back. "Let's just pool our money together, *again,* and hammer everything into shape and fill 'er up with rocket fuel and take a day trip to the Dominican Republic."

Mace's smile weakened. Dex was reminding him that they were both totally out of money. It was true: there would be no more TURBO racing.

"I will pay you back," Mace told Dex. "Every cent you loaned me so we could do this."

"You're out of your mind," said Dex. "I got every penny's worth out of our venture. You don't owe me anything."

Mace chuckled dryly. "I don't even have enough money to get out of Cuba."

"Let's just stay here," Dex suggested. "We can start a lounge act."

"Hold on," Aya said. "You won the Prix! There's HUGE cash in that!"

Mace cleared his throat. "Not when I reveal myself, and the world discovers I'm only twelve."

Aya's eyes bugged out of their sockets. She sprang to her feet. "Why would you do that?"

He sighed. "I have to, Aya. I'm underage. Winning illegally isn't winning at all."

"But *you* came out on top!" Aya argued. "Without cheating. You can't help your age. Own your win, dude."

"I don't know," Mace said. "I figure I'm just getting

started. I'll enter the junior circuit. Work my way into the sport the way all other pro TURBOnauts do."

They sat in silence, watching reporters and agents and event coordinators frantically running up and down the cobbled streets shaded by unhappy-looking trees. Aya was deep in thought, troubled.

"I'll get you guys home," Aya offered.

"I wasn't . . . I didn't mean to ask . . ."

She stopped Mace. "I know. Forget about it, though. What? I'm going to let you guys stay stranded here?"

"What about you?" Mace asked. "What's next?"

Aya grew serious. "I'm going to keep racing," she said. "You've got your Glove. I still want a shot at it."

"That's fair. If I reveal myself, I'll leave you out of it."

"Mace, we're better than the junior circuit." She nudged him with her elbow. "Maybe I can convince my parents to sponsor two or three cryptics."

Another reporter stormed past, speaking into a headset. "The police are reporting two versions of *Continuum*! Yeah, a look-alike! No. No. It hasn't turned up. Probably some crazy cosplayer superfan for all we'll ever know. Nope. Just some hired pit-crew types, and they don't know squat. The chief mechanic was in Mexico City. On his way, yeah, but he's not going to know much. I hear he was fired before launch. Of course. I will!"

The one-sided conversation drifted out of earshot. The reporter absently stepped in a deep pothole filled with brown water and cursed.

"You going to put them out of their misery?" Aya asked Mace. "The authorities should know what Tempest was up to."

Mace cleared his throat. "She's still out there."

Tempest. Her advice rang in his ears. . . .

Keep your mouth shut. Anything you say will only come back to haunt you.

He thumbed the memory chip in his pocket. His get-out-of-jail-free card. But he wouldn't dare hand it over, not yet. Not without knowing her next move. She could still cause Mace and his family serious trouble if she wanted to. The flight recorder was his only protection. The only way he could be sure she'd leave him alone.

He had crossed the finish line first. But their battle had ended in a draw.

Not a bad chess game, really, for a pawn taking on a queen.

"If I reveal myself, the press is sure to uncover some of Tempest's plot on their own. As long as I'm masked, justice won't come. Not fully."

"As long as you're masked," Aya argued, "you're safe. You're in control of what happens next. Come on. We can race for a few more years under our helmets, then reveal the truth after. I'm going to want a rematch, you know."

Mace nodded, listening. She was making a tempting point.

Someone stopped in front of them on the sidewalk, staring down at them.

Mace looked up. It was Henryk.

Hands in his jean pockets, his red hair purposefully messy, he leaned against a tree trunk. "Hey," he said.

"Hi," Mace and Aya and Dex said back.

"Congrats on the win, Renegade. You earned it."

"Thanks," Mace replied dryly. He couldn't tell if Henryk was being authentic or spiteful.

Henryk cleared his throat. "Do you guys accept apologies for what they're worth—or does there have to be some kind of chicken dance first? Either way, let me know. I'll do it."

Mace raised an eyebrow. That sounded pretty genuine.

"Chicken dance! Yes." Dex nodded enthusiastically. "You may begin."

Mace reached over and slapped Dex's shoulder.

Some people passed through their conversation, walking at a clip. Henryk waited for them to go by, scratching his spindly goatee. "Well, um," he cleared his throat. "I'm sorry."

Aya urged him on with a wave of her hand. "Go on. Sorry for . . . ?"

"I'm sorry for getting caught," the redheaded Viking said.

Quick as lightning, Dex removed a boot and threw it at Henryk's head. He ducked. It struck the tree behind him with a thud.

"I was joking." Henryk laughed, throwing his hands up defensively. "I was JOKING! Jeez."

"Never mind. Um, where were we?" prompted Mace.

Dex retrieved his boot. Henryk released a deep sigh. He looked his rivals in the eyes. "No, really. I'm sorry. I am. I've been a jerk, okay? I let Tempest turn me into a cheater and I cheated and I even almost killed Talon and then I almost got killed myself. And I'm sorry. It wasn't worth it—not by a long shot."

"I dunno," Dex turned to the others. "Did that sound good enough to you?"

Mace shrugged. "Not sure. Maybe that chicken dance is in order, after all."

Henryk looked at each of them, hope draining from his face. "Are you serious?"

"Chicken dance!" they all three chanted together.

Henryk began, slowly at first, to tuck his hands under his armpits and lift his knees while erratically bending over. He made a squawking sound and picked up speed.

"Now eat twenty breakfast burritos," Mace called out.

Everyone laughed.

Henryk scratched his head when it was all over. "I'm off, you guys. I'm heading home to Norway and I think I might just retire from TURBO racing. But good luck with whatever's next for you all. I promise your secrets are safe with me. Cool?"

"We're cool," Mace told him. "You might want to sing 'I'm a Little Teapot' to Talon, though." They watched him walk down the sidewalk with his head hung low.

"The ceremony starts in fifteen minutes!" someone shrieked, sprinting past. "Where's Renegade? Brahma and

Nazaryan are already on the stage. SOMEONE PLEASE FIND THE CHAMPION!"

Champion, Mace thought. *How 'bout that?*

He rubbed his eyes. He felt suddenly exhausted. "I'm going up to my room."

"Mace," Aya pleaded. "If you go up to the podium, keep your helmet on. You won, fair and square. You deserve the purse. You deserve to keep racing."

"Maybe," Mace said. He wasn't sure what he'd do. The Golden Glove came with *a lot* of cash. But covering up his age just for the money—that was selling out. And he'd learned his lesson on that, big time.

Aya stopped him from rising. "Hey, Mace?"

"What is it?"

"No matter what: You did it. You beat her."

Mace smiled. "Yeah, *we* did, didn't we? It feels good! But, you know, here we are." He lifted his hands wide, slapped them back down at his thighs. "And now what?"

"Who knows? We'll see!" Dex said. "Make every morph matter, right?"

Mace thought about that. "Make every morph matter," he agreed.

///// CHAPTER THIRTY-EIGHT

Mace struggled to his weary feet and made his way back upstairs to Team *Trailblazer*'s suite. He slipped quickly into his dark-blue-and-orange flight suit and fitted his helmet snug over his head. He stepped out into an empty hallway and headed back outside.

The crowds and the media noticed him. They swarmed.

Mace saw his friends just in time to give them a final nod. They gave him a thumbs-up, and then his view of them was blocked.

"Renegade! Renegade!" they chanted. The throng parted

a little, and he was granted a path across the street and over to the stage.

Aya wanted him to stay anonymous, so that no one would challenge his right to the Glove. But, then again, coming clean might allow him to own his win in another way.

A twelve-year-old! Jax Anders would go hoarse screaming it. *A seventh-grader! Coming out of nowhere and winning the Prix! The Gauntlet Prix! Can you believe it, maniacs? Mace Blazer is his name!*

He didn't know what he was going to do.

Akshara and Taz were on their podium steps, waving to the crowd. The middle pedestal—the highest of the three—was unoccupied. Mace took his place there, turned, and raised his hands high in victory. The crowd lost it. His fellow TURBOnauts on either side of him clapped. Mace took their hands in his, and together they raised their arms. Confetti flew through the air. Camera flashes blinded him, even through the visor.

Suddenly, a hush fell over the crowd, a thick blanket of silence. TURBO Association president Linda Gimbal walked down the lush red carpet in the center of the plaza. Mace's heart began beating faster, and his breath caught. Gimbal presented Akshara and Taz with large medallions in silver and bronze, which they gladly accepted, and then all eyes were upon Mace. The Glove—known officially as the Golden Gauntlet—drew closer. Closer. Gimbal took the waiting trophy from its bearer and turned to face the champion.

Time seemed to stop as she held the Golden Gauntlet up. A speech was made. Jax Anders appeared and made some comments to the crowd. Mace didn't remember any of it. His eyes were on the prize.

It was perfect. Awesome. Gleaming and golden, with a flawless shine.

Linda Gimbal presented the Golden Gauntlet to him. He took it.

It was heavy, consisting of countless interlocking metal plates. Mace slipped it over his left hand, a sense of accomplishment enveloping him. He flexed his fingers and then made a fist. The Glove was surprisingly limber. And then the sound of clapping came, followed by whistles and shouting. Mace pumped his gloved fist in the air, as he'd seen every TURBO champion before him do.

The silence returned, and the American national anthem filled the square. Mace put his free hand over his heart and sang the lyrics along with others in the crowd.

When it was finished, the reporters gathered like bees around an intruder and he barely had time to process any of the questions.

"Who are you? Will you ever show yourself to the public?"

"Give us clues. Are you male or female?"

"Tell us more about how you feel. Are you proud? What will you spend all that *money* on?"

"Do you have any family who know who you are and are watching you right now? How do you think they feel?"

Mom. Dad. Mace thought of them, watching this unfold from Miami. He could almost see their proud, beaming smiles through the camera lenses. He thought of the Gerbers, and of Mr. Hernandez, and of his friends who were here, but off in the background, against the hotel wall. They couldn't be up here with him because it would reveal too much.

"Do you have any new sponsors lined up?"

"They've named your winning maneuver the Renegade Roll. Care to comment?"

"Will you ever take off that helmet?"

Without realizing what he was doing, Mace used his free hand to loosen his chin strap.

The world instantly fell silent as a tomb. Mace heard the distant hum of power generators throughout Havana, and nothing more.

Everyone leaned in and waited.

Jax Anders stared at him, frozen, genuine excitement dawning on his features.

He heard a single male voice shout from the back of the crowd. Dex. "Do what you know is right, Renegade!"

And then a girl's voice rose in sudden, unexpected agreement, "It's okay! Go for it! Show them just how much you love this sport!"

Mace's eyes pooled up with tears. Aya—after all they'd been through—had his back. She and Dex both did. He realized that others would too. *Doing the right thing could sometimes feel lonely,* Mace thought. *But if you make a habit of it, maybe you can blaze a trail for others to follow.*

Mace took a deep breath. "Ah, screw it," he muttered. He seized his midnight-blue helmet by the chin and lifted it off his head.

ACKNOWLEDGMENTS

Racing is a team sport, and so is writing a novel. I am incredibly grateful to a number of brilliant people for their roles in getting this book out of the gate and across the finish line. To my HarperCollins crew chief, David Linker, thank you for believing in this project and for giving it wings. Paul Lucas, I'm grateful to have you as my wingman. Thank you so much for being there for me over the long haul! I owe many thanks to John Fischer and Alli Dyer, as well. I especially owe a debt of gratitude to Pete Harris. Pete, I can never thank you enough for getting me behind the wheel of this thing and for pumping it full of high-octane fuel! To all of you, what an honor this ride has been!

Author Ryan Dalton, thank you for your early feedback and for cheering me on. Mom and Dad, I am grateful to you both in more ways than I can say, but you get a special shout-out here for boosting my research efforts by taking me and the kids to NASCAR races and providing me with VIP pit access. Those experiences were instrumental for me. And finally, to my wife and kids, Clare, Ariel, and Everest, thank you all so much for enduring the very real burdens you have borne on account of this marathon journey, and for providing me with that infinite well of encouragement and support that every author secretly needs and that this author not-so-secretly demands during his frequent moments of doubt. I love being able to write, and I'm eternally grateful to you three for the countless ways in which you make that possible.

I also want to thank my readers. Book readers are the best! Yes, I'm talking to you. Thank you so much for taking this tale for a spin. I am forever grateful for your enthusiasm and support, and for the time we've spent together. I'm hopeful that we'll enjoy many more thrills, you and I, as our paths continue to cross.

Lastly, I'd like to note that within these pages I've paid homage to a few of my favorite popular culture references. If you recognize a turn of phrase or two, please know that I've borrowed them out of sheer reverence, and do not claim them as my own.

Mace's adventure continues in

//TURBO_RACERS//
//ESCAPE
/////VELOCITY

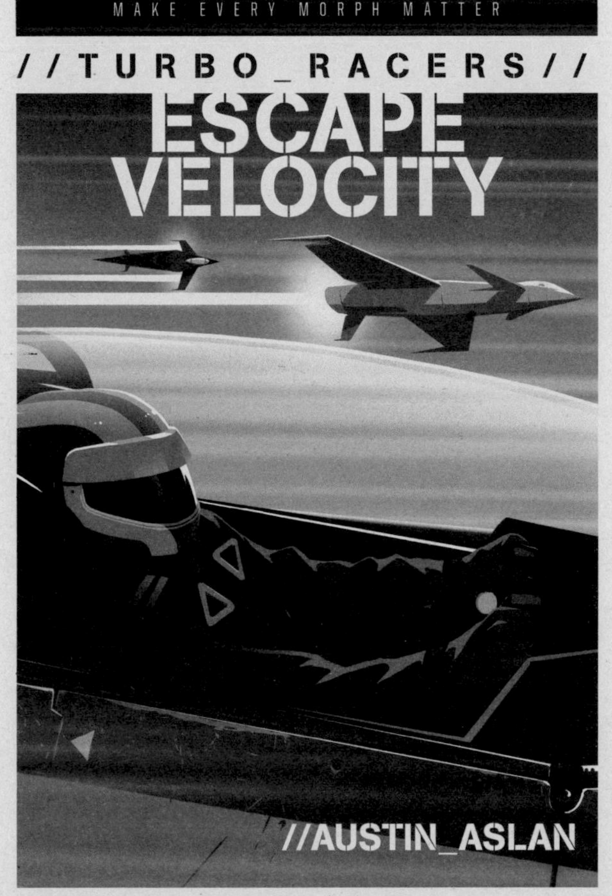

Read on for a sneak peek! ///////////////

CHAPTER ONE /////

Trailblazer shot out of the Cairo Formula 1 stadium in fourth place, a blue-orange streak ready to morph to air where the road turned to dunes. Mace Blazer gripped the steering wheel, looking for a way to dart past hometown hero Ibrahim al-Aswani. The pilot of gold-red-and-green *Horus* was proving difficult to overtake. And farther ahead of al-Aswani: Darwín Maldonado of *Evolución* and *Lotus*'s Katana.

The final lap through the Egyptian capital city was underway. Mace hadn't dropped below fifth place today. But he hadn't held the lead, either. *Horus* was taking full advantage of its home turf. And Mace had underestimated the tenacity of Maldonado, who had been trading the lead with Katana and eluding Mace all afternoon.

"I'm not worried. Am I worried?" Mace asked his comm.

"You're worried. Just a little," Dex suggested in his ear.

"I am?"

"This'll be over in ten minutes. You're half a mile behind *Evolución*. If you're not making up four and a half feet per second, you won't take the flag."

"Oh, so I should go faster?"

"That might help," Dex replied helpfully. "You might also ask everyone—nicely—if they wouldn't mind slowing down."

"Tried that once," Mace confessed. "Wasn't very effective."

Trailblazer transformed from a roadster into a jet and launched over the dunes into the blue. The air segment was a short hop over a sprawling landscape of tall brick buildings and towering turrets and minarets. Mace mentally mapped out his course over the city bedlam to the ancient Nile, where his morph into the not-so-deep river would require a precise angle, just a smidge steeper than a plane touching down on a runway.

He set his sights on *Horus* and laid into the throttle—but just a little—and climbed past the Egyptian local and into third place. He checked his rear displays. *Guillotine*'s French phenom Leon "Napoleon" Dubois—a distant threat in fifth—was only now rising into the air, cutting left into the helicopter course, where he could engage Katana directly.

Dicers, as they were known, couldn't accelerate as fast as fixed-wing craft, but they could take turns as sharp as bats in a cave. So dicers separated from the pack during air transects, branching onto shorter, curlicue courses and giving audiences a close-up thrill.

Katana was already weaving her dicer, *Lotus*, through a series of canyonesque Cairo streets. Mace had a good view of his rival friend from his higher altitude and noticed her rounding a corner with too much caution. "That's my shot!" Mace cried.

"Finally," Dex agreed, "Aya made *one* mistake."

"That's one more than me." Mace accelerated, feeling the powerful engine behind the cockpit drawing in a greedy breath of air. His own weight against the seat back seemed to double. Blood pooled at his feet; his vision grayed. The smart cushioning squeezed his legs in response, pushing oxygen-rich blood back up into his core, and his eyesight recovered.

And then just as quickly, he decelerated, banking sharply to draw parallel with the river. The negative g's sent his stomach into his mouth. He battled a wave of nausea but maintained control.

It worked. The water entry was flawless—and he dropped below the Nile's surface just ahead of Aya, denying her second place. "Now that's what I call denial!"

"Nope." Dex's voice was dry. "No 'da Nile' jokes on my watch."

"But I waited over two hours to drop that line!"

"My contract specifically stipulates I don't have to hear puns from you."

"You're no pun. You're no pun at all."

"Shut up and finish the job, Mace."

The race flowed against the river's current, which slowed everyone down. Aya began to gain on Mace, and he felt a stab of concern. He needed to keep a healthy margin ahead of her; she'd be a threat later on, no matter what. After all, five races into the season and she'd only bested him in the first matchup, taking silver in Shanghai when he'd taken bronze. She was ravenous for an outright win. But so was Mace. A checkered flag today would put him one race away from securing a berth in his second Gauntlet Prix. Qualifying for the championship race so early in the season would really take the pressure off and keep the Association off his back for a while longer.

Technically, Mace was too young to race in the pros. But the league knew if they pulled Renegade from the lineup while he was hot, the fans would lose their minds.

So winning was a matter of survival—it was the only way he could stay in the sport. The fame and the glory and the money were just perks.

Mace would race for free, of course, but he wasn't going to let anyone know that.

He throttled up, and the turbine responded beautifully. "Mace, watch your gauges," warned Dex. "We're getting feedback from the combustor sensor."

I know. That's on purpose. Dex didn't realize that *Trailblazer*'s engine was operating at 100 percent capacity, because Mace had forgotten to tell anyone that he and the trimorpher and a box of tools had had a tinker party last night.

The extra *oomph* he'd engineered was perfectly legal, but risky. The history of racing has forever been a dicey dance between power and panache, after all. Mace hadn't utilized *Trailblazer*'s extra kick yet. But this was the last lap, and he was behind.

Aya inched up on him, slowed, then fell away. Mace exhaled a sigh of relief. He backed off the throttle just enough to stay ahead of her. *Trailblazer* trembled, as if frustrated at backing down, hungry to unleash her full potential. Mace was aware of another racer pushing through the water just behind Aya. Additionally, *Flipside* and *Pendragon* were passing him on the river's surface. Those two were impossible to best on the water, but Mace let his anxiety roll over him. He'd retake the skimmers—the speedboaters—on the other terrains. He always did.

"Your morph's coming up. After an elbow turn. Water-to-ground. Make it matter."

Mace saw the bend, nosed sharply, and punched it for the ramp. His morph to ground was solid, and he took off along the wide-open highway toward the Great Pyramids.